Scandal at Riverside High

Tenure

_____

Demetrius Smith

Scandal at Riverside High

Copyright © 2017 by Demetrius Smith

are copyright protected and are the property of its owners.

ISBN-13: 978-0692828083

ISBN-10: 0692828087

Dedication

This project is dedicated to my son, Caleb, and my daughter, McKenzie (Mac). "Never stop exploring the boundaries of human expression."

MACALEB ENTERPRISE, LLC

Acknowledgments

With warm and sincere thanks to Willie Wilchie IV, my lieutenant and brother from another mother. Thank you for believing in me and this project from the very beginning. Special thanks to the cast and crew of Scandal at Riverside High for your commitment and hard work. Thanks to my mentors, Tyrone Moore, Elbromoe Nod Ibrahim and Al Malone, for your guidance and shared wisdom. Thanks to my family, friends, and to the community of Riverside in South Memphis. My gratitude is also extended to MonTrelle Arnold, Riki Jackson, and Joshua Libertine.

According to the Center for Sex Offender Management, females account for around 10 percent of all sex crimes reported to American authorities. However, a much higher percentage –over 30 percent of all teacher-student sexual offenses in the US are estimated to have been perpetrated by females.

In the latest available statistics, in 2014, just under 800 school employees in the US were prosecuted for student sex crimes: around one-third of them female.

Thank you for your support

Visit and like us on

Facebook: scandal at riverside high

Or visit our website:

www.scandalatriversidehigh.com

This story was inspired by true events.

"Let me reassure you all that my commitment to Riverside remains solid, and to those who worked so hard to close our doors, I must respectfully say to you, Riverside yesterday, Riverside today, and Riverside forever!"

Juvenile Detention Center, Memphis, Tennessee

In a small, damp visiting room, Edward Jones and his wife, Frances sit silently across the table from Carlos, their teenage son. Dressed in a disheveled orange jumpsuit and handcuffed to the table, Carlos avoids eye contact with his parents. There is a noticeable black circle around his eye, and his top lip is slightly swollen. His father slides a book across the table to him. The title reads: 'The Autobiography of Malcolm X.'

"What's this?" Carlos asks.

"What does it look like?"

"It looks like you want your only son to be a racist."

"Are you stupid, or just stupid? Which is it, son?" He shakes his head in frustration. "I have an idea. How about, we let the world know that I raised a wannabe pimp and thug. For God's sake, boy, you could be in here for murder!"

Frances rubs Edward's arm soothingly. "Remember your blood pressure," she says.

"Let me ask you a question. Has she even tried to contact you?" Edward asks.

At that very moment, Carlos has a flashback of himself standing at the detention center pay phone attempting to make a call only to receive an automated voice operator. *"The number you have reached, is no longer a working number."*

"I didn't think so," his father taunts. "See, son, black folks can't be racist. You must have the privilege and the power to be a true racist. Look around you. Does it look to you like we have either one?"

"Edward, you know we should have never allowed him to live with your brother," Frances interrupts.

"It's not his fault, Ma," Carlos says.

"You damn right it's not!" his father shouts. "This sits squarely on your shoulders. Which is why you have only two options; show us you can change."

"Or?" Carlos asks.

Edward removes a brochure from his inside jacket pocket and slides it over to him. The brochure reads: *"Harden Military Academy."*

"Military school!" Carlos shouts.

"You got it," his father replies. He stands. "You better pray he lives; because if he doesn't, you won't have any options. Let's go, baby."

With tears in her eyes, Frances stands. She gives a deep sigh. Edward walks to the door, peeps through the square glass and taps to alert the guard. Carlos's mother hurries to his side and gives him a kiss on the cheek.

"I love you, baby. Everything is going to be alright," she says.

The guard opens the door.

"Let's go, Frances!" his father yells.

She reluctantly tears herself away from Carlos and rushes to the side of her irritated husband. As they exit, the guard enters, unshackles Carlos from the table, and escorts the watery-eyed teen back to his cell.

Riverside campus, main entrance, the school marquee reads: "Riverside High - Home of the Mighty Rams; Annual Honors' Day program, May 15, 2014." Each year at this time, the honors award ceremony is a staple event at the school and has been since its doors opened in 1957. Riverside was molded as a public institution designed to even the playing field in education for blacks during the Civil Rights era. Its long list of distinguished graduates includes pastors, city officials and police officers, just to name a few. Although the school boasts of a noble past, unfortunately, its future is not as bright. Riverside was one of twelve local-area schools on the School district's priority list recommended for closure. The recommendation to close twelve schools came after an informal proposal that the district shutter up to 12 schools to help eliminate a budget gap and avoid cuts to programs that keep students in the district. Finishing at the bottom five percent of the state's performing schools, severely under-enrolled, with at least 1,100 seats open, the decision appeared inevitable. However, due to an outcry and a community proposal to improve Riverside, the board was prompted to allocate funding out of its eight hundred-million-dollar budget to keep the school open for another year extending the school's lifeline, while allowing those community leaders to make good on their proposal. Despite the looming cloud that hovers and the uphill battle ensuing, the students, faculty, and alumni refuse to allow the recent set of unfortunate developments tarnish this year's awards presentation.

Meanwhile, in the teachers' lounge, across the hall from the school library, a copying machine clamors as it prints out sheet after sheet, which reads *"Quiz."* Mr. Patterson, the twelfth-grade English teacher, anxiously awaits the last document to print. He then removes the stack of papers and exits the lounge. Two male students hurry past him.

"Let's get to homeroom, fellows." Patterson admonishes.

"Yes sir," they both reply.

Seconds later, he passes the yearbook film room and sees Carlos fumbling with items inside his gym bag. On the desk, alongside the bag sits an expensive looking camera. Unaware of the teacher's presence, Carlos carefully places the camera inside of the bag. Intrigued, Mr. Patterson decides to observe his odd behavior for a few seconds longer.

"What is this boy up to now?" he mumbled to himself. "Carlos, shouldn't you be in the auditorium!"

A startled Carlos panics. "Huh? He quickly zips the bag. "I mean, yeah." he says. I'm on my way there now."

Tossing the bag strap across his shoulder, Carlos exits the room. As he passes by Mr. Patterson, the two exchange disapproving glances. Mr. Patterson shakes his head in frustration and then proceeds to his classroom. Just as he reaches his door, science teacher, Ms. Wiggins, whose classroom is located across the hall, is just about to close her classroom door.

"Good morning, Mr. Patterson," she says.

"Good morning, Miss Wiggins," he replies.

She observes the stack of papers he is holding. "A quiz? Seriously? You're giving a quiz the last week of school?"

"Yep."

"Wow. Your students must really love you."

He smiles. "No, not really," he says. He laughs and then enters his classroom.

Before closing her door, Miss Wiggins can't help but stare at his sturdy robust physique and shake her head in admiration.

Downstairs, in the office of guidance counselor, Ruth Banner, the commotion of the day's events are far removed from her mind as she stands next to a large window overlooking the school's rear parking lot. She's holding a card which reads:

To: Ruth Banner

"Congratulations on a job well done. Your father would be proud."

Signed:

Superintendent Stockton

With her chest thrust out and a wide smile on her face, Ruth basks in the moment. Her moment is short-lived as her attention is drawn to the parking lot. She sees Carlos as he appears in view carrying the gym bag. He hastily approaches an early model Chevy, opens the trunk, and he places the gym bag inside. He then darts back toward the building. Ruth's eyes follow his every step until he disappears behind the corner of the building.

In the school auditorium, the band is getting in a last-minute rehearsal before the assembly program begins. The side door of the auditorium abruptly opens, and Carlos enters. The band stops. Everyone turns in his direction. Mr. Ford, the band director, gives him a grim stare. Realizing he has broken Mr. Ford's main rule about band members reporting on time; Carlos stands there looking like a deer caught in the headlights.

"Carlos, so glad you could join us," Mr. Ford says.

"My bad, Mr. Ford. I had to shit, I mean I had an upset stomach," Carlos replies.

Some band members burst into laughter.

"Quiet down!" Mr. Ford shouts. "If you would please spare us the particulars and join us."

Carlos hurries over to the band. He grabs his drum and places the strap around his neck.

In the main office, the schools' Principal, Dr. Lanier sits solemnly at his desk with his elbows on top and hands clasped vibrating against his chin. He stares at the wall directly in front of him, which displays a picture of his mentor, the very first Principal of Riverside, J.L Coleman, Sr. Beads of sweat congregate at the base of his grey hair. A manila envelope with the words, *"For Your Eyes Only"* written across the bottom is placed squarely in front of him. Suddenly, secretary Tuggle's voice blasts through the intercom snapping him out of his trance.

"Dr. Lanier, the announcements." she says.

"I'm coming," Mrs. Tuggle," he replies.

He takes the envelope, opens the top drawer of the desk and shoves it inside. He removes his two-way radio from his desk. He stands and walks toward the door leading to the front office. He attempts to call out on the device.

"Coach, what's your twenty?"

He curses beneath his breath once he realizes that the device has no charge. Inside the front office, he slams the device down on the charger startling Mrs. Tuggle.

"What's the problem?" she shouts.

"Have you seen Coach Curry!" he yells.

"No, I have not," she snaps back. She hands him the announcements. "However, if it keeps you from having a heart attack, I will go and fetch him for you."

Ignoring her request, he takes the announcements and walks over to the intercom. Just before he takes the microphone, he is filled with remorse.

"Please, accept my apologies," he says. "I'm not sure what got into me."

"Um huh," she replies and rolls her eyes.

Dr. Lanier clears his throat.

"Good morning, teachers and students. As I know you are all aware, we will be conducting our honor's day program this morning."

Upstairs, in a secluded corner of the school library both Coach Curry and the school Librarian, Belinda Nelson are busy conducting an assembly of their own. With her arms wrapped around his neck, and her legs straddled around his waist, he has her pinned against the wall. They pant and kiss as they vigorously attempt to undress one another. He grabs her by the neck exposing his wedding ring. Suddenly, they stop, startled momentarily by the voice of Dr. Lanier. Their panic turns to embarrassing laughter when they realize that it's only the morning announcements.

"We will be on an abbreviated class schedule. All students are to remain in homeroom. No student should be roaming the halls without a pass. Coach Curry, would you report to the main office please?"

The two finish their episode and quickly help one another get dressed.

"Coming, master," Coach sarcastically remarks.

"He's under a great deal of pressure," Miss Nelson admonishes. She straightens his collar. "He could use a friend right now."

"Friend? No, what he needs is an assistant principal," Coach says.

"Is it really that bad, Greg?" Miss Nelson asks.

"Is it bad? He orders me around like he's the one doing me a favor."

"Well, you are a certified administrator. So, apply for his job."

"I don't want the job." He pulls her close. "I'm the coach."

"And a damn good one," Miss Nelson says.

"You better believe it. All that matters to me is winning another state title."

"Is that all that matters to you?" She taunts.

"You know what I mean," Coach replies. "I can't be an effective coach if I'm chasing hoodlums around this campus all day. Besides, it's his own fault the school is failing. It may be time for him to step aside and let someone else have it. It just won't be me."

"I hear you. So, are we still on for this weekend?" Miss Nelson asks.

"About that, we will have to make it another time."

She pushes him away. "But you said..."

"I know what I said. It's just that things are a bit complicated at home. I need you to be a little more patient."

"Patient? I have been nothing but patient, Greg."

"Listen," he says as he pulls her close. "In a couple of weeks, Sabrina is planning a trip to St. Louis to visit her parents. I can find a way to get out of it. I'll play sick or something. Then she and the kids can go without me, and you can have me all to yourself."

Miss Nelson rolls her eyes and slightly turns her head. She has heard this line before she thinks to herself. Coach takes his finger and places it under her chin, turning her face back towards him.

"We good?" He asks.

"Yes. We are good," she says, giving him an accommodating smile.

"That's my girl. Now, if you will excuse me, I have to go and help a friend."

He kisses her on the cheek, releases her and quickly exits the library. Miss Nelson can only swallow her pride and watch him leave.

"What a life," she mumbles.

Back in the school auditorium, the band is finishing up a number.

"Now, you are starting to sound like a real band," Mr. Ford says. "Let's take a short break. I want everyone back here in twenty minutes."

Band members unman their instruments and barrel out of the auditorium. Carlos walks past Mr. Ford.

"Where do you think you're going, Mr. Jones?" he asks.

"I thought we were taking a break."

"The rest of us are taking a break. According to you, you've had a restroom break already. Now, have a seat."

Baring his teeth but realizing that he is about one hundred pounds outmanned, Carlos reluctantly takes a seat in the first row.

Back in Ruth's office, she sits quietly behind her desk scanning through the school's yearbook. Suddenly, she is interrupted by a female student.

"Good morning, Miss Banner. Could I get you to help me?"

"Yolanda!" Ruth shouts. "How is our class Valedictorian?" "Please come in."

Yolanda enters. "I'm so nervous," She says as she hands Ruth a pearl necklace, then turns around.

Ruth begins securing the necklace around Yolanda's neck. "You will do just fine. How is your mother? I bet she is excited."

"She is beside herself. You would think she is the one graduating. She has called my entire family and she made them promise to attend my graduation."

"Believe me. This moment is just as special to her as it is to you.," Ruth says. "Now, turn around and let me look at you." Yolanda complies. "You Just remember. If you begin to fall apart up there, locate your mother's face in the crowd. A mother's encouragement can help pull you through any situation. "

"I will," Yolanda replies.

They hug. "You look fantastic by the way." Ruth says."

Thank you for everything."

"You're welcome. Now, you run along. You have a speech to give, young lady."

"Ok. See you later?"

"Sure."

Ruth escorts her to the door. Yolanda waves good-bye, as she walks away. At that exact moment, a few male members of the band exit the boy's rest room. Ruth spots Chris, a tall and lanky band student. She waves in a shameless attempt to get his attention. He pretends not to see her. She waves frantically, until he has no choice but to acknowledge her. He gives an uneasy smile and nod. She beckons for him. He gives a quick scan of the perimeter, then inconspicuously walks over to her.

"Hey, Miss Banner. What's up?" Chris asks.

"Hi, Chris. I have something I want to show you. It will only take a moment."

"Ok, but I can't stay long. Mr. Ford hates it when band members are late."

"It will only take a second. Come in."

Chris scans the hall before following her inside. Ruth eagerly walks over to her desk and opens the top drawer. She reaches in and pulls out a small box.

"Now, I know what you're going to say, but please don't be upset. I just could not resist."

She opens the case exposing a shiny silver class ring with a clear setting.

"Do you like it?" she asks. "I even had your initials engraved." She points.

"Miss Banner, I told you. You don't have to buy me things. You've done so much already," Chris replies.

"I know. You said no more gifts. I promise. This is the last one."

She removes the ring from the box. Anxiously, she reaches for his hand. He reluctantly concedes. She places the ring on his finger.

"I don't know what to say," Chris says. "Thanks. It's really nice."

Seconds seem like hours as she and Chris stand in awkward silence.   With a huge smile, Ruth intimately stares at him.

"Well, I guess I should go," Chris says as he slowly turns to exit.

"Chris," Ruth says.

"Yeah?"

"Could I have a hug?" She asks.

His smile slowly dissolves, and his muscles tighten. Before he can give his consent, Ruth rushes towards him. She grabs and hugs him so tightly that it is hard for him to breathe. She places the side of her head on the center of his chest, and then inappropriately rubs her hand up and down the center of his back. Chris is paralyzed with fear.

"You smell really nice," she whispers.

Chris squirms free from her grasp. "I have to go now," he replies. "I really don't want to be late."

He turns and dashes for the exit. Ruth stands there with a mischievous grin as if she had somehow won him over.

Later, in the school auditorium, the program is minutes from starting. Students, visitors and dignitaries file into the auditorium. During the band's downtime, Carlos catches a glimpse of the ring on Chris's finger, which he is keenly aware was not there before.

"That's a nice ring, home boy," Carlos says.

"Oh, thanks," Chris nervously replies. He quickly offers up an explanation. "It was a graduation gift."

"Is that, right? So was mine," Carlos replies.

He holds up a fist exposing his ring which identical to the one Chris is wearing. Not sure of his intent, Chris dismisses the incident as a strange coincidence.

"Great minds think alike, huh," he says.

"I guess so," Carlos replies.

He suspiciously smirks at Chris, who returns a nervous smile.

Later, during the program, Yolanda is at the podium giving her speech.

"I would like to thank my teachers, my family and friends for all of your love and support. I don't believe I would be standing here today had it not been for each one of you."

The crowd applauds.

"Lastly, I want to thank God for giving me such a loving and supportive mother. Although you made it seem easy, I know it was anything but easy. Mother, you raised three kids alone. You're my hero."

The crowd gives a thunderous applause. Yolanda's mother, seated in the center aisle, begins weeping uncontrollably. Ruth, standing alone in the rear of the auditorium, becomes overwhelmed with emotion. She exits the auditorium into the lobby, removes a napkin from her purse and wipes her tears. As she gathers herself, Miss Nelson arrives suspiciously late and approaches Ruth.

"Hey you. What's wrong?" she asks.

"You know how I get at these things," Ruth replies.

"Oh, come here you big wuss!" Miss Nelson gives her a hug, and they both laugh.

"So, where have you been hiding?" Ruth asks.

"Oh, well, you know. Uh, I had some last-minute stuff to do. A librarian's job is never done," Miss Nelson stutters.

"I see," Ruth replies.

"Never mind where I've been. You know what I want to know."

"If you are referring to my trust fund money, then yes, the money hit my account this morning," Ruth replies.

"Good! I could use a loan," Miss Nelson says. "I'm only kidding. So, what are you going to do with this year's proceeds?"

"Well, the first thing we must do is celebrate."

Ruth reaches inside her purse and hands her the letter from the superintendent congratulating her.

"Oh, my God! Congratulations! Look at you! Have you told your mother?" Miss Nelson asks.

"Not yet, I plan to visit her after school," Ruth replies.

"I wish I could be there to see the look on her face. She is going to be so proud of you."

The women are suddenly interrupted by the audience's thunderous applause coming from inside the auditorium.

"We had better get in there," Miss Nelson says.

The women enter the auditorium trying not to draw attention to themselves. Dr. Lanier is now standing at the podium to address the crowd.

"Thank you," he says. He holds out his hands, quieting the crowd. *"You may be seated.*

"You know. A dear friend asked me the other day if I had to do it all over again, would I choose to become an educator. I gave his question some serious thought. Although it is true, those of us in the field of

education don't make the money that some people make in more glamorous careers. However, money aside, I am convinced that there is no greater purpose in life than to answer the call to nurture and develop our nation's future leaders. I received that call over thirty years ago; Answering that call gave my life purpose. As I look at these bright and beautiful young people sitting here before me, I am filled with optimism and hope for our country's future. I would have to say to my friend: No. I wouldn't change one thing about my life or my choice to help build this nation's future."

The crowd applauds.

"Thirty years is a lifetime." He pauses to reflect. *"I have so much to be thankful for. I have been blessed with a beautiful wife, a wonderful staff, and a community of loyal parents, alumni, and community leaders whose undying support has carried me this far. Riverside is not my school; you're my family,*

and there is nothing stronger than family. He pauses. *This is difficult," he mumbled softly into the microphone.* He pauses once more. His hesitation begins to make the crowd anxious. *"I have come to a pivotal moment in my life," he says. "Which has caused me to have to make a very important decision. I can't think of a better time or place to announce that I will not be returning to Riverside next year. I am officially retiring, effective at the conclusion of this school term."*

The audience blares out a resounding moan. He turns to his wife, and she responds with a startled expression. At the rear of the auditorium, Ruth emotionlessly looks on. Miss Nelson glances over at Coach Curry. He shrugs his shoulders; indicating that he was unaware. Carlos lowers his head in a shameless attempt to conceal his smirk. Mr. Patterson sitting with his homeroom gives, Dr. Lanier an incredulous stare. Dr. Lanier holds out his hands, quieting the crowd once more.

"Let me reassure you all that my commitment to Riverside remains solid, and to those who worked so hard to close our doors, I must respectfully say to you, Riverside yesterday; Riverside today; Riverside forever!

The crowd jumped to their feet and gives a roaring applause.

****

Later that afternoon, at Pine Meadow Retirement home, Ruth's white sedan pulls into one of the facility's parking spots. She grabs her purse, quickly exits the car, and heads straight for the entrance. The automatic door opens, and Ruth enters the lobby. A small elderly lady with a cane and a slight hunch, greets her at the entrance.

"Ruth, how are you dear. How is your mother? We really miss her at bingo," she says.

"Oh, hi, Ms. Rosenthal. I'm fine. Mother's diabetes is a constant struggle, but I'm sure she misses bingo as well."

Ruth attempts to walk away; Ms. Rosenthal grabs her wrist.

"Sweetie, do you think I could trouble you for a small loan?" she whispers.

"I really don't think that's a good idea, Ms. Rosenthal. Maybe you should lay off Bingo for a while."

Ms. Rosenthal rolls her eyes, snaps her neck, and scoots away. Ruth chuckles.

"Was it something I said?"

Hoping not to be bothered by another one of her mother's friends needing money, Ruth picks up the pace and briskly heads to the elevator. She impatiently presses the up-angle button continuously. The door finally opens. Ruth rushes inside and presses the third-floor button. Moments later, she exits the elevator and darts straight to her mother's apartment. She uses her key to let herself in.

"Mother!" she yells.

"I'm in the bedroom, dear!" her mother yells back.

Ruth enters the bedroom and tosses her purse on the dresser. She is surprised to see a uniformed black man standing at her mother's bedside.

"Oh, Hello. I'm Ruth Banner," she says.

"Hello. I'm Larry Williams. Pleased to meet you," he replies.

"Are you the cable guy, Larry?" Ruth jokes.

He laughs. "Oh, I get it, Larry," he says. "No, actually, I'm here installing your mother's new emergency response system," he replies. "You're the schoolteacher?" he asks. "Your mother hasn't stopped talking about you."

"I'm a guidance counselor actually," Ruth replies.

"Wow, that is impressive. I don't know how people like you do it. I mean working with those kids and all. I can hardly stand my own kids, let alone someone else's kids. Well, I've got you all set up Ms. Elaine. I just need your signature, and I will be out of your hair."

"I hope that thing won't start screaming in the middle of the night and gives me a heart attack," Elaine says. "My daughter will sue the pants off your company."

She snatches the clipboard from him, signs it and gives it back.

"Mother! Be nice."

"Not to worry; the only way it can be activated is by you," Larry says. He hands Elaine the emergency response necklace. "If you should have an emergency, just push this button. You can wear it around your neck or hang it on your bedpost if you like."

"God, forbid I should wear that dreadful thing around my neck," Elaine replies.

She takes the necklace and tosses it next to her on the bed.

"Well, it was nice meeting you both. I will let myself out."

"It was very nice meeting you," Ruth says. She shakes his hand.

As he leaves, Ruth stands there with her eyes locked in on him as he leaves. Her mother grunts loudly to regain her attention, then beckons her over to her bedside. Ruth quickly kneels beside her mother's bed and grabs her mother's hand.

"I am so glad you came when you did. I didn't trust that man," her mother says.

"Oh Mother, he seemed pretty nice to me."

"You never know. Besides, I didn't want that stupid machine anyway."

"If you didn't want it, why on earth did you order it?" Ruth asks.

"I didn't. It was that black director girl. She's making everyone get a unit installed. I bet she is getting a kickback. They work together you know?"

"Is that so?" Ruth sarcastically replies. "Well, anyway, that's not what I want to talk to you about. I have some great news mother."

"Do tell," her mother says.

"I've finished my administrative course work. That means I can apply for a school of my own. Isn't that fantastic?"

Ruth releases her mother's hand, stands, and walks over to the dresser. She picks up a picture of her deceased father. Less enthused, her mother looks on.

"I only wish Daddy were here. He would be so proud."

Ruth places the picture back on the dresser and returns to her mother's bedside. She kneels once more.

"So, what do you think? Aren't you proud of me, Mother?" she asks.

"Of course, I'm proud," her mother replies. With a hesitant low tone, she mumbles, "It's just that--

"What is it, Mother?" Ruth snaps.

"Well, I thought you liked being a guidance counselor."

Ruth immediately becomes irritated. Her voice elevates.

"Why do you always do this, Mother? Why can't you just be happy for me!" She shouts.

"I am happy for you, dear," Elaine replies.

"I know if Daddy were alive, he would be very happy."

"Your father and I were both proud of you, sweetie," Elaine says. She rubs her fingers through Ruth's hair to quell her temper. "You remind me of him. You both share the same optimism for life. So, what are your plans?" Elaine asks as she tries to appear supportive.

"Well, it just so happens that Dr. Lanier is retiring, and there is a good chance I could replace him," Ruth replies.

"What! My daughter, principal of that zoo! Over my dead body!"

"Mother! Riverside is not a zoo."

Ignoring Ruth, Elaine points to the nightstand. "Hand me my phone book," she says. "Where are my glasses?"

Ruth reaches for the book, and glasses, and she hands them to her.

"You remember my church member, Doris?" Elaine asks. "Her son Herbert is the principal at this new charter school."

"I'm not sure," Ruth replies.

"Of course, you remember," she says as she flips through the pages of her phone book. "You met him last year at the church Christmas party. Remember?"

"Oh, right, I do remember. He seemed a little creepy. Doesn't he still live at home?" Ruth asks.

"He looks after her. He is a good son, and he is single."

"That is very flattering." Ruth cringes. "What does all this have to do with me?" she asks.

"If I recall, Doris mentioned that he needed an assistant principal, and they are very nice people," her mother replies.

Ruth's face tightens. "So, again, what does this have to do with me?" she says.

"Trust me. This is a far better opportunity for you. These are the type of people you should get more acquainted with."

"You mean, white people?" Ruth asks.

"Yes, if you want to hear the truth."

Ruth leaps to her feet.

"Let me give you a dose of truth, Mother. I'm not interested in any charter school, and I'm certainly not interested in hobnobbing with your snobbish friends."

Ruth grabs her purse from the dresser and walks out.

"Ruth! Don't leave! I just want what is best for you."

Ruth stops and returns to the bedroom.

"You mean, what's best for you? I make a real difference in the lives of those students. You have never understood that."

"I just feel that you get too involved with those kids, that's all," her mother says.

"Oh God, not again! Yes Mother. I made one mistake, and you won't let it die. Why can't you see that I have learned my lesson?"

"Have you Ruth? Have things really changed?"

Ruth's eyes become cold, hard, and flinty. She growls, stomps her feet, and storms out.

Later, on the drive home, Ruth reflects on the wonderful relationship she shared with her father when he was alive, the softness of his touch and kind words that would always make her feel better whenever her life was spiraling out of control. Oh, how she longed for those days. He never judged her or made her feel as though she couldn't do anything right. Which is a very different relationship she is now left to endure with her mother. Try as she might, as far back as she could remember, she has been helpless to break the spell that her mother casts over her.

As she arrives home, Ruth pulls into her driveway. She exits the vehicle and walks up the walkway to her front porch. She checks the mailbox and retrieves the mail. She hurries up the steps, then unlocks the front-door. As she enters the house, she pauses. She notices food wrappings on the dining room able. She can hear the sound from the television coming from her bedroom. Certain that she turned it off that morning before she left for work, she is prompted to investigate. Immediately. She heads down the hallway. She reaches the bedroom door, stops for a second, and takes a deep breath. She then bursts through the door. Stunned, but not completely surprised, she finds a shirtless Carlos there sprawled across her bed aiming his camera in her direction.

"Smile Principal Banner!" Carlos yells. He snaps a shot of her with his camera.

"Carlos, how did you get here, and where is your car?" she asks.

"My car broke down today, so I had my uncle drop me off," he replies.

"Tell me you are not being serious right now?" Ruth says.

"It's cool. I told him this was the home of one of my honeys from school. He don't suspect nothing."

"He believed you?"

"For a forty ounce and a nickel bag, he could care less. Which reminds me, my money is running out. When do a brotha get paid?" he asks.

"You will get your money," she replies.

She tosses her purse on a chair next to the bed, and leaps across his body into bed; they cuddle.

"Good, because I would hate to think I was getting played," he says.

"Oh, sweetie, you know I would never do that," Ruth replies.

"Tell you the truth, watching that hypocrite's face today, hell… I would have done it for free."

"I don't know. I feel kind of bad for him," Ruth says.

"Seriously! Why in the world would you feel sorry for him?" Carlos replies. "He treats everyone like shit; especially you."

"I'm going to wash your mouth out with soap. Besides, you're just still upset over that suspension?"

"You damn right I am. He knew how important that track meet was for me. All the scouts were there."

"You still have a year of eligibility," Ruth says.

"That's not the point, and why you trippin?" he replies. "This was your idea. Remember?"

"I'm not tripping," Ruth says. She sits up and engages him directly. "It's just that I don't know how long Mother will be with me, and daddy never got to see me run my own school."

"If you ask me, you care too much about what your mother thinks," Carlos replies.

"Well, I didn't ask you, did I?"

"Whatever mane," he says.

Carlos pouts, and they both disengage from the conversation. He sits up on the edge of the bed, bends over to retrieve his shirt from the floor, and begins to get dressed. Once dressed, he grabs her purse and begins to ramble through it.

"I'm out," Ruth says. "I smoked the last one on my way home."

Carlos removes her car keys.

"I'll be back," he says.

"Could you at least put gas in it this time?" Ruth asks.

"Sure," he replies.

He removes money from her wallet, winks at her, and exits the room. Ruth sighs heavily.

"You sure know how to make a girl feel special!" she yells.

Ruth listens attentively as the car's engine starts. The sound becomes more distant as Carlos backs out of the driveway. Believing that the coast is clear, she excitedly removes her cell phone from inside of her purse; she then leaps back into bed, pulling up a downloaded photo taken of Chris, she places one hand inside of her panties and begins shamelessly pleasuring herself.

The next day at Ruth's home, she is sitting alone at the dining room table. She is enjoying a cigarette while flipping through a magazine. Her phone rings.

"Hello. Yes. This is Miss Banner." She stops turning the pages. "Oh, hello!" she shouts. "Yes, I can be there." She pauses. Her face lights up. "Ten o'clock; thank you. Thank you very much. I'll see you then. Good-bye."

She hangs up the phone and then lets out a loud scream.

The following morning, at a nearby hotel, Dr. Lanier, in his suit and tie sits solemnly at the foot of the hotel bed. With both hands tucked under each thigh, he stares at his reflection in the mirror. Next to him sits an open briefcase and inside is the manila envelope along with his wedding band. The fizzling sound of water can be heard coming from the bathroom shower. He checks his watch and, then retrieves his ring and places it on his finger. He closes the briefcase, picks it up from the bed, stands and heads toward the exit. Before leaving, he stops at the bathroom door, slightly opens it and yells inside, "I'm headed to my meeting."

He closes the bathroom door and exits the hotel room.

Later, that same morning at the Board of Education, Ruth steps out of the elevator into a hallway. There are at least half a dozen offices located on the floor. Unsure exactly where to go, she scans the directory on the wall. She spots her target. An arrow points right, directing her to the Office of the Superintendent. She immediately heads in that direction. With only a few minutes to spare, she approaches the secretary's desk.

"Good morning. I'm Ruth Banner. I have a ten o'clock appointment with Superintendent Stockton," Ruth says.

"Good morning. Yes, he is expecting you. Go right in."

Ruth smiles, and walks over to the superintendent's door. Before entering, she pauses, and double checks her outfit. She takes a deep breath then opens the door. Inside, the superintendent stands to greet her.

"Miss Banner!" he shouts. "The gang's all here. Come in and join us."

Ruth's eyes widen and her heart rate increases when she sees Dr. Lanier at the conference table alongside a young African American female. She attempts to keep a neutral facial expression as she slowly walks over and takes a seat across from everyone. The superintendent takes his seat.

"Well, you don't need much introduction I suppose. You already know Dr. Lanier," Superintendent Stockton says.

"Why, of course I do. Good morning, Dr. Lanier," Ruth faintly replies.

"Good morning, Miss Banner."

"This bright young lady is Mrs. Diana Meeks," Superintendent Stockton says.

Ruth flashes a pasted-on smile. "Good morning, Mrs. Meeks." "It's nice to meet you."

With a wide energetic smile, Diana energetically extends her hand across the table.

"Good morning, Miss Banner! It's a real pleasure to meet you," she replies in an overzealous tone. They shake hands.

"Before we start, tell me Miss Banner. How is your mother?" Superintendent Stockton asks.

"Mother is struggling a bit with her diabetes," Ruth replies. "I'll tell her that you asked about her.

"I'm so sorry to hear that, but yes, please, give her my best."

"I will."

"Great. Now, let's get to it. I know you must be wondering why I called you here to begin with?" Superintendent Stockton says.

"Yes sir. I must say that I was completely blind-sided by the phone call."

"You are not the only one here blind-sided. I assure you Miss Banner. Isn't that right, Dr. Lanier?" Superintendent Stockton taunts.

"I suppose that is true, sir," Dr. Lanier replies with a chuckle.

"Mrs. Meeks, did you know Miss Banner's father was a principal for many years?" Stockton asks.

"Is that so?" Diana replies. "Yes," Ruth proudly interrupts. "He was a true professional," Stockton says. "Who, I might add, would have never decided to retire without at least giving his boss a proper notice. Isn't that right, William?"

"Touché, sir," Dr. Lanier replies.

Superintendent Stockton laughs.

"Oh, I'm just pulling your leg, William. Things won't be the same without you. I'm sure Miss Banner would agree."

"I certainly do."

"However, it's like my father would always say. When one door closes, another one opens."

"That's a very good philosophy sir," Ruth replies.

"Indeed, it most certainly is. Despite our comrade's bad timing Miss Banner, he has proven not to be the kind of man who would abandon his post without an exit strategy. Which brings me to the reason I called you here today."

Ruth immediately sits upright in her chair, crosses her legs, and clasps her hands. Her feet bounce uncontrollably under the table.

"Me, sir?" she asks.

"Miss Banner, I need your help as we begin to write a new chapter at Riverside," he replies.

"Whatever I can do to help, I'm willing to do sir."

"Now, that's the spirit." He pauses. "Miss Banner, I need you to help mold the future."

Unable to endure the suspense any longer, Ruth leaps to her feet.

"I accept the challenge sir!" she shouts.

"Fantastic!" he replies. "I didn't expect such a fiery response to the call to duty, but I will take it!

Miss Banner, please help us welcome Riverside's new principal."

Diana leaps to her feet and smiles directly at Ruth. Suddenly, Ruth's posture stiffens. Her heart rate rises. The loud thumping of her heart drowns out all other sounds. She can see the superintendent's mouth moving, but his words are falling on death ears. A few seconds' pass, and gradually her focus begins slowly reappearing. Now, the words are clearer.

"Dr. Lanier and I couldn't think of anyone more qualified to help Mrs. Meeks adapt to this new challenge," Stockton says.

"I've explained to Mrs. Meeks just how valuable your assistance has been to me during my time at Riverside," Dr. Lanier interrupts. "Don't worry Miss Banner. I'm a fast learner," Diana says. Ruth stands silently as everyone volleys for her attention. Seconds go by. Awkward tension fills the room. Ruth's dazed and unresponsive reaction causes everyone to become a bit concerned.

"So, what say you Miss Banner? Can I count on you?" Superintendent Stockton asks.

"I, uh, yes. I mean, yes sir. of course, you can count on me," Ruth stutters.

They all breathed a sigh of relief as the tension is released.

"Wonderful! I knew you would not let me down. I assure you Miss Banner; your dedication won't go overlooked. You remind me so much of your father. He was a team player as well," Stockton says.

With a saccharine smile and faint tone, Ruth replies, "Thank you, sir."

"Well, that's settled. We can consider this meeting adjourned. Dr. Lanier, may I have a word please?" Superintendent Stockton beckons him over.

The two men separate from the women to engage privately in dialogue. Diana walks over to Ruth and attempts to strike up a conversation of her own.

"I was thinking. Maybe we could have lunch one day this week," She says.

Still appearing a bit shell shocked by the news, and anxious to distance herself from the scene, Ruth slowly replies, "Lunch... Yes, lunch, sure. I will give you a call. Will you excuse me?" She turns to leave.

"Miss Banner," Diana hands Ruth her card. "You're going to need my contact information."

"Oh, yes. Thank you." Ruth takes the card from her. "I'm not sure where my head is. I will call you."

Ruth then hurries out of the office. Dr. Lanier, sensing there is a problem, interrupts his conversation with the superintendent.

"Could you give me a second, sir?" he asks.

He then follows off behind her. Ruth instinctively feels him getting closer, so she picks up her pace. He catches up with her at the elevator. Slightly short of breath he barely manages to get the words out.

"Miss Banner, may I have one second please?"

"I am really in a hurry, Dr. Lanier. Can this wait some other time?" she asks.

Frantically, she begins pressing the down button.

"Are you ok?" Dr. Lanier asks.

"Yes, I'm fine," she replies. "I hope you have a wonderful retirement."

The elevator doors finally open. Ruth rushes inside. She turns and they lock eyes. The elevator doors slowly close.

Minutes later, in the parking lot, Ruth unlocks her car door and flings her body inside. She tosses her purse on the passenger seat. After sitting in a quiet daze for a few seconds, she explodes in a fit of rage, slamming her hands against the steering wheel and releasing a gut curling scream.

****

Later that day, at an auto repair shop, Carlos is sitting inside his car blasting rap music. His pinched facial expression reveals that he is unhappy with the sound quality of his stereo. Glancing in his rear-view mirror, he spots Ruth's vehicle pull up. He mutes the music and exits the car. He yells over to a couple of mechanics under the hood of another vehicle, "I'll be right back!"

The mechanics spot Ruth sitting inside her vehicle. They exchange questionable glances, smile and shake their heads. Carlos enters her car.

"How did it go?" he asks.

"Horrible! It was just awful!" she replies.

"What happened?"

"I didn't get the job. That's what happened!"

Carlos slams his hands against the dashboard and bounces his head back against the headrest.

"Who did?" he asks.

"Some young black girl who Dr. Lanier recruited. She couldn't be much older than you. It's like they were just sitting there waiting for me to come and make a fool of myself."

"I don't understand. Why did they call you?" he asks. Momentarily ignoring him, she wipes her tears, and begins to search through her purse. She takes out her cigarettes and lights up. Carlos anxiously awaits her reply. She takes a drag and exhales.

"Would you believe they want me to mentor the little brat?" she says. In despair, Carlos slumps down in his seat and slowly digests the bad news. Suddenly, as though struck by lightning, he jumps up and immediately goes on the defensive.

"You don't think they suspect anything, do you? My daddy would kick my ass."

Ruth exhales again. "No," she replies. "You don't have to worry. No one suspects anything."

"Cool," Carlos says. He relaxes. "So, what are you going to do?" he asks.

"I just need some time to think," she replies. "I stood there smiling like an idiot and gave the superintendent my word that I would do it."

Ruth takes a few more drags on her cigarette. Emotionally drained by the day's events, she attempts to change the subject.

"So, what's the word on your car?" she asks.

"It should be ready this week," he replies. "It's gonna be a little more than I thought though."

Ruth exhales smoke and gives him a suspicious look.

"How much is a little more?" she asks.

"About two hundred dollars."

"Jesus, Carlos!" she shouts.

She takes another long drag off the cigarette and puts it out in the ashtray. Shaking her head, she grabs her wallet from her purse, removes some cash, and hands it to him.

"This should take care of it."

"I need to get high," Ruth says. "Are you done here?"

"Naw, I still got some stuff to take care of. I can get my uncle to drop me off later."

"Is that really a good idea, Carlos?"

"I told you mane. I got this. I'll bring the weed."

Carlos opens the door. Before he exits, he leans over and kisses Ruth on her cheek. Ruth's cell phone rings.

"Hello. What! I will be right there!"

Ruth arrives at her mother's Retirement Home. She storms inside the apartment in a panic.

"Mother!" she shouts.

She enters the bedroom and there, she finds her mother in bed being attended to by the staff nurse.

"What happened?" Ruth asks. "The emergency response center phoned me."

With a very weak voice her mother replies, "I'm fine, dear."

"Your mother injected a little too much insulin, which caused a downward spike of her blood sugar levels," the nurse interrupts.

"Why on earth didn't you get someone to help, Mother?"

"I misread my dosage. I wasn't wearing my glasses."

"She is stabilized," the nurse says. "I'll monitor her tonight." She rubs Elaine's arm. "It sure is a good thing you had your emergency response system, Miss Banner."

"Huh," Elaine shirks.

"Thank you," Ruth says.

"You're welcome," the nurse replied. "I'll be in the next room, if you need me.

Ruth walks over to the bedside and runs her fingers through her mother's hair.

"You scared me half to death," she says.

"Don't worry about me," Elaine replies.

"You're all I have. It would kill me if something were to happen to you."

Elaine gives a slow, weak smile and nods her head. Suddenly, her eyes widen, and she glances up at Ruth.

"I almost forgot. How did your meeting go? Did you get the job?" she asks.

"Oh, things went well," Ruth responds while avoiding eye contact. No decision has been made. I'm definitely being considered for the position."

"That's good, dear," her mother says.

Ruth's smile slowly dissipates as her mother relaxes.

In a restaurant the following day, a waiter approaches Ruth. "Would you like to order now?" he asks.

"I'm expecting a couple of people. You can bring us all a glass of water with lemons," she replies.

"Yes mam"

A few seconds later, Diana appears at the front entrance. She spots Ruth, smiles, and walks over to the table. "Hi, Miss Banner. Sorry I'm late. I'm still learning my way around the city."

"Good afternoon, Mrs. Meeks; no worries."

The waiter returns with the water.

"Here we are," he says.

"Oh, thank you. I don't like lemons," Diana says.

Slightly annoyed he concedes. "Ok. One water, no lemon. I'll be right back."

Ruth spots Miss Nelson at the entrance, and she holds up her hand to get her attention.

"Is someone else joining us?" Diana asks.

"Yes. Miss Nelson, the school librarian. I hope you don't mind. She is dying to meet you."

"No, of course I don't mind."

Miss. Nelson approaches the table. "Hello, ladies."

"Hey you." Ruth replies.

"Miss Nelson, this is Diana Meeks, our new principal."

Diana stands and extends her hand. "It's a pleasure to meet you, Miss Nelson."

"My God! You're just a baby," Miss Nelson blurts.

"No. I am an adult."

"I see," Miss Nelson says.

The women take their seats. Awkward tension mounts, and Ruth couldn't be more pleased with the unpleasant exchange.

"Forgive me. I didn't mean to be so rude." Miss Nelson says." "No. I understand. I graduated high school at 16. I hate when I get that response from people. You would think I would be used to it by now."

Miss Nelson grabs Diana's hand. "There is no need to explain. Your folks must really be proud of you. So, where are you from?" she asks.

"I was born and raised in Dallas."

"Really?" Ruth interrupts. "Were you raised in a two-parent household?" she asks.

Stunned by Ruth's brashness, Miss Nelson presses her lips together in a slight grimace.

Diana almost chokes on the sip of water. "Uh, yes ma' am. As a matter of fact, I was," she replies. "My father is an engineer, and my mother is an investigative reporter for a local news station."

"Dallas, now, that's a nice city," Miss Nelson says.

"Were there no principal jobs in Dallas?" Ruth asks.

Equally stunned by Ruth's onslaught, Miss Nelson clears her throat, and quickly attempts to deflate Ruth's question before Diana has a chance to respond.

"I think what Miss Banner is trying to say is that one would think that a progressive city, like Dallas, would have more to offer an intelligent young lady such as yourself." She then gives Ruth a stern look.

"That is what you meant; right, Miss Banner?"

"Yes. That's exactly what I was trying to say," Ruth replies.

"I guess we have Dr. Lanier to thank for that," Diana says.

"How do you know Dr. Lanier?" Miss Nelson asks.

"We met last summer at a conference in Dallas. We had dinner and talked for hours. We found that we both share the same passion for education. A few months ago, he contacted me and told me about his plans to retire."

"So, then, you haven't known him very long?" Ruth interrupts.

"That's right," Diana replies. "Imagine my surprise when he asked me if I wanted to succeed him."

"You must have left quite an impression on him," Miss Nelson says.

"I guess so. Strange thing is, I haven't been able to reach him since our meeting with the superintendent. Have either one of you spoken with him?" she asks.

"No. I haven't heard a peep from him," Miss Nelson says.

She then glances over at Ruth, who just shrugs.

"Nope, not a word," Ruth says.

"That's strange," Miss Nelson replies. "So, Mrs. Meeks, do you have any children?

Diana reaches inside her purse, retrieves her cell phone, and pulls up a family photo. She eagerly passes the phone to Miss Nelson. "That's my son Caleb, and my husband, Arthur."

"You have a lovely family. How old is your son? Miss Nelson asks.

"Thank you. He is eight months," Diana replies.

"May I take a look?" Ruth asks.

Miss Nelson passes the phone to her. She takes a quick look, gives a squint, and passes the phone to Diana.

"Your husband, is he an educator as well?" Ruth asks.

"No. Arthur majored in information technology," Diana replies. "God only knows how I wish he was in education. It would simplify our lives. He worked for a small start-up company back home."

The waiter returns and begins distributing the beverages.

"It was quite noble of him to quit his job to support your career move."

"Well, the plan is for me to support the family while he interviews. He really wants to start a small business. I don't think now is the right time."

"This generation sure has a different way of doing things," Ruth says.

"Really? How?" Diana asks.

Miss Nelson narrows her eyes at Ruth, cautioning her. Ruth ignores her.

"Forgive me, but my mother was a wonderful homemaker. My father supported the family. It just seems to me that a young wife and new mother would put more priority on family life."

"Waiter, we are ready to order now!" Miss Nelson interrupts.

With a slightly bruised ego, Diana, quickly responds. "Education is my passion. I consider myself very blessed to have a husband who supports me. Besides, I'm sure things were very different in those days."

"Why don't we look at the menu?" Miss Nelson interrupts hoping she can help avoid another tense exchange between the women.

Everyone sits quietly for a moment. While they study the menu, their waiter returns.

"What are we having ladies?" he asks.

"Could you bring us a bottle of wine?" Miss Nelson replies.

"Wine, at this time of the day?" Diana says.

"It is early, Bea," Ruth says.

"Both of you, just hush. I think we all could use a relaxer. Bring the bottle sweetie. It doesn't matter what it is," she says.

"Sure." The waiter replies.

Later, after completing their meals, and downing a few glasses of wine, the mood is much more relaxed.

"That steak was delicious," Miss Nelson says. She attempts to pour more wine into Diana's glass.

"Oh, no. No more for me, thanks," Diana responds.

'How about you, Ruth?"

"I'm done thank you.

"Suit yourselves," Miss Nelson says. She pours herself another glass.

"I'm going to have to run a few more miles tomorrow. I don't normally eat this much during the middle of the day," Diana says.

"Oh, so that's your secret," Miss Nelson replies. "I was wondering how a woman who recently gave birth, could maintain that figure.

"Thank you," Diana says. "Arthur and I ran track in college. It's definitely hard, but we both try to get the gym time in."

"Well, Ruth and I are Zumba girls. Aint that right Ruth?" Miss Nelson says.

Ruth just smiles at her.

"Really? I've never tried that. I bet it's fun," Diana replies.

"Class meets tomorrow night at six. Why don't you join us?"

"I would love to."

"Would you believe Miss. Banner has lost over sixty pounds."

"Wow! Are you kidding me?"

"It's true. Thanks to Zumba and a tummy tuck," Ruth responds.

"Well, count me in for Zumba, but hold the tummy tuck," Diana jokes.

Holding up her glass, Miss Nelson gives a toast. "Zumba for three!" she yells. They toast.

"Oh, wait. I forgot. The house is a mess," Diana interrupts. "We are still moving in. I would hate to bail on Arthur."

"I'll tell you what, how about Miss Banner and I come by tomorrow and help you get the place together? " Miss Nelson says. With the three of us working hard, we should be able to make Zumba by six."

Completely caught off guard by the suggestion, Ruth takes a big gulp of water then widens her eyes at Miss Nelson.

"No. I couldn't ask you to do that," Diana says.

"That's nonsense. We will be glad to help. What time should we be there?"

"Well, Arthur has a ten o'clock interview."

"Great. Say, ten thirty? Text your address to my phone before we leave," Miss Meeks says.

"This is awesome. I don't know how I will ever repay you guys."

Meanwhile, Coach Curry enters the restaurant, with his wife and two small children.

"Hey, Isn't that Coach?" Ruth asks.

Miss Nelson abruptly turns in his direction; she quickly turns back around in her chair, slightly slanting her body away from the view of Coach. The hostess escorts the family to their seats. Coach spots the women and gives a nod and pasty smile.

"Is he a coach at Riverside?" Diana asks.

"Yes, he is. He led both the boys' basketball and track teams to state championship titles for two years in a row," Ruth explains.

"Wow? That's impressive."

Miss Nelson becomes stiff and suddenly disengages from the conversation. Boiling with anger, she begins drinking heavily. The women take notice, but don't pry. Coach excuses himself from his family and heads over to the table.

"Good afternoon, ladies," he says.

"Hello, Coach," Ruth replies.

"Coach," Miss Nelson grunts.

"Coach Curry, this is Diana Meeks, our new principal," Ruth says.

Diana in true form, leaps out of her seat and extends her hand. With an incredulous stare, he quickly gives a stiff smile. He shakes her hand.

"Uh, this is a pleasant surprise," he says.

"I hope we can count on a third championship," Diana jokes.

"We certainly intend to do just that," he replies.

Coach releases her hand, and Diana takes her seat.

"Miss Nelson, would you mind if I have a quick word please?" Coach asks.

Without uttering a word, she abruptly stands and follows him. They reach a secluded area in the restaurant, just out of view of his wife and kids.

"Where the hell did, she come from?" he whispers. "I have neck ties older than that girl."

"It shouldn't be a problem for you, Greg. I believe she is about the same age as your wife. Who, by the way, I thought was in St Louis? At least now, I know why you haven't returned any of my calls. I'm such a fool," she mumbles.

"I was going to call you when I had a free moment," he says. He firmly places both hands on her shoulders and looks directly into her eyes. "Sabrina decided at the last minute, to postpone the trip."

"What are we doing, Greg?" she asks. "You don't owe me any explanations. Go back and be with your family."

She abruptly walks away.

"Bea, wait a second," Coach says.

She ignores him and continues to the table.

"Is everything ok?" Diana asks.

"Everything is fine," Miss Nelson replies. "Are we ready to leave?"

"Yes," Ruth says. "Mrs. Meeks has requested that we give her a walk-through of the campus and don't worry about your bill. I paid it."

"Thanks. Let's do it. I could use some fresh air."

Later that afternoon, at Riverside, the women stroll down the hallway.

"So, what do you think, Mrs. Meeks?" Miss Nelson asks.

"It's amazing. It's much larger than I expected," she replies.

"Yep, it is pretty big," Miss Nelson says. "It's just too bad that we have more school than students."

Just as the ladies reach the lobby near the main office, to their surprise, they run into Mr. Patterson.

"Hey there!" Miss Nelson shouts.

"Hello, Mr. Patterson," Ruth says.

"Good afternoon, ladies," Mr. Patterson warmly greets them.

"What are you doing here? I thought you would be out saving souls this summer," Miss Nelson jokes.

He laughs. "I just dropped by to get my mail."

"Well, lucky you. You get to meet our new boss. Mrs. Diana Meeks, this is Mr. Patterson; oh, wait, forgive me, Reverend James Patterson."

Diana becomes visibly nervous as she makes firm eye contact with the handsome young teacher. She extends her hand. He takes hold of it. Embarrassed by the moisture swiftly building in her palms, she quickly retrieves it, folds her arms, and inconspicuously attempts to stroke them dry against her triceps. Ruth and Miss Nelson exchange questionable glances.

"It's a pleasure to meet you," she says.

"Likewise; I only wish we could have met in a more professional setting," he replies.

"There is something to be gained by informal meetings. I mean, it often allows us to get to know the real person," Diana says.

"I never thought about it like that," he replies.

She continues the small talk, hoping that she can divert everyone's attention off her obvious attraction to him.

"So, you're a minister?" she asks. "That's wonderful. We need more God-fearing men in education. So, where is your church?"

"I'm an assistant pastor, actually. I was just recently ordained. Guess you could say I'm starting a new career as well."

"Mr. Patterson is also the English department's chairman," Ruth interrupts.

"Really? I'm an English major," Diana says.

"Well, if that is the case, let me go on record and say that I wouldn't object to a little favoritism when the budget is dispersed next year," he jokes.

Diana squeals out an embarrassing laugh. Miss Nelson lifts a single eyebrow at her. Ruth lowers her head, smirks and rubs her neck.

Mr. Patterson chuckles. "Right, well, Christ Holiness on South Third is my church home. I would love for you all to visit sometime."

"I will be sure to come," Diana says. Quickly realizing her oversight, she corrects herself. "I mean, we will. My husband and I will attend."

"Great; I look forward to seeing you both there. Now, if you ladies will excuse me, I really must get going. Have a great summer."

"Have a good summer," Miss Nelson says.

"Bye, bye," Ruth says.

The women all stand there, in a moment of complete silence. Diana feels compelled to make light of the awkward tension she has created.

"He seems nice," she says.

With a raised eyebrow, Miss Nelson, bursts into laughter. "Yes, he certainly is. So, how about we peek at your new office?" Miss Nelson asks.

"Oh, yes!" Diana shouts.

"I don't know if that's a good idea, Miss Nelson. Shouldn't we have Dr. Lanier's permission?" Ruth interrupts.

"We're just going to take a little peek inside. I'm sure he wouldn't mind. He is the one who recruited her."

They enter the office. Diana's face beams with pride. She walks toward the center of the room, then suddenly stops and pirouettes. Ruth stands near the door's entrance with her arms folded and jaws tight.

"Wow!" Diana yells. "I can't believe it."

She walks over and takes a seat in Dr. Lanier's chair. She places her purse on top of the desk, then rubs the palm her hands across the smooth surface.

"You look right at home, Mrs. Meeks. Wouldn't you say so, Miss Banner?"

"Yes, right at home," Ruth replies. She grinds her teeth.

Diana reaches inside her purse and retrieves her wallet. She removes a family photo.

"Miss Banner, I know you are over the yearbook staff. So, could I get you to do me a huge favor?" she asks.

"Favor? I'm not sure what you mean," Ruth hesitantly replies.

"Would you have this copied and enlarged?" Diana asks. She hands Ruth the photo. "I want it for my new desk."

Ruth's muscles tighten. She gives a forced smile, then walks over and takes the picture from Diana.

"Sure," Ruth replies. "After all, I am a team player."

****

Later that night, at Diana and Arthur's home, Arthur does sit-ups on the bedroom floor while, next to him, entertaining himself, is Caleb kicking and punching his musical playmate. Diana sits at the foot of the couple's bed attempting to make a phone call.

"Leave a message?" Arthur says.

"I've already left three. I'm not leaving another one," she replies.

"I'm sure he will call soon," Arthur says.

She hangs up the phone in frustration. "I don't get it. For months, I can't get Dr. Lanier off the phone and now that I'm here, he disappears."

"Maybe he is on vacation," Arthur speculates. He finishes one last sit-up. He picks Caleb up off the floor and places him in his crib. "Give him a day or two."

"Maybe you're right," Diana agrees.

Arthur takes a seat next to her on the bed, as Diana becomes distracted in her own thoughts.

"So, how was your day?" he asks.

"My day?... Oh, I'm sorry," Diana replies. She redirects her attention. "It was great, actually. I toured the school. I even got to see Dr. Lanier's office; or, my new office."

"Was it everything you envisioned?"

"It was amazing. Miss Nelson, the school librarian, and Miss Banner were very encouraging. Well, Miss Banner, not so much, but that's another story. Which reminds me, they are coming by in the morning to help me with the house."

Arthur laughs, then kisses her on the forehead.

"Look at you, on the job one day, and already got the staff during personal favors. You're in the big league now, sweetheart," he jokes.

"Ha, for your information, they volunteered," she replies. "My question is, are you ready for your interview tomorrow?"

Arthur becomes slightly annoyed by the question. "If you mean, am I prepared to go punch the man's clock. Yeah, I'm as ready as I will ever be."

"Please, don't go there. We've discussed this already. Now is just not a good time to start a business," Diana says. They both climb into bed.

"I know. I know. You don't have to give the speech," Arthur says.

"Thank you. I promise, once we figure things out financially, then we can reconsider the idea." They cuddle under the covers. "We still don't have a baby-sitter, remember. God only knows how much that's going to cost us," she says.

"That's true."

She kisses him. "So, how was your day?"

"I met our new neighbor today. He and his wife are having a fight party Friday night, and we're invited."

"A fight party? I don't think so. You can go. I'll watch Caleb."

"He invited us both. What would I look like showing up without you?"

"You know how I hate violence. Just tell them that I didn't feel well or something."

"Yes ma'am," Arthur snaps.

"Really? I know you're not sulking," she says. "Besides making new friends, how was the rest of your day?"

"Oh, yeah, wouldn't want to leave out the highlight. My dear old mother-in law called," he says.

Diana abruptly sits up. "Oh, no!" she shouts. "I was supposed to call her tonight. It completely slipped my mind." She quickly glances at the alarm clock. "It's late. I'll have to call her in the morning. So, what did she say?"

"Oh, nothing but the usual conversation; have you found a job? Is my daughter still supporting you? You know, just being her warm and loving self."

Diana laughs, then cuddles up with Arthur again. "I'm so sorry you had to go through that baby. Really, I am," she chuckles.

"Oh, so you think that's funny."

He tickles her, and they both laugh. Suddenly, they are interrupted by the ringing of Diana's cell phone.

"Wait! Wait!" she shouts. "That may be Dr. Lanier."

Arthur reaches for the phone. "It is a local number," he says.

"Answer it!".

"Hello. Yes. Who may I ask is calling? Hold one second."

"Who is it?" Diana asks.

"It's a Mr. Patterson," Arthur whispers as he covers the receiver with one hand.

"Mr. Patterson?"

Confused, nevertheless intrigued, Diana beckons for the phone.

"Hello. Good evening to you." She pauses. "Is that so?" Diana raises an eyebrow at Arthur. "Yeah, now is not the best time. Can I get back with you? Thank you. I will. Goodnight."

Diana hangs up the phone, and hands it back to Arthur. He places it on the nightstand.

"Should I be jealous?" Arthur asks.

She shakes her head in disbelief.

"Get a load of this," she replies. They get back under the covers. "Miss Banner gave one of the teachers my number and encouraged him to contact me so that we could discuss the English department's budget for next year. I haven't seen a budget for next year."

"And he thought it was a good idea to call at ten o'clock?" Arthur asks.

"Apparently so," she replies.

"That's odd," Arthur says.

Diana sinks down into Arthur's chest and sighs. "Do you think I'm in over my head?" she asks.

"Stop that now. he reassures her.

"You were born for this,"

She kisses him. "Thanks. I needed that" she says.

"Besides, you can't quit. I don't have a job, and Lord knows we can't move back to Dallas to live with your parents," he jokes.

Diana laughs. "You know you're crazy, right?"

They begin passionately kissing, before being interrupted by Caleb's crying. Diana pushes Arthur away, and tosses back the covers.

"Mama's here, boo," she yells.

"No. No," Arthur begs. He playfully reaches for her. He grabs her arm and attempts to pull her back into bed.

"Daddy has some more issues he would like to discuss."

The following day at Diana and Arthur's home, Ruth, Miss Nelson, and Diana are hard at work organizing the couple's kitchen.

"All I'm saying is, why is it that black schools seem to have such a difficult time securing proper funding? You have overcrowded classrooms and underpaid teachers multi-tasking. It's a mess," Miss Nelson says.

"I have explained it to you already, Bea," Ruth replies. "Funds are distributed per the student-teacher ratio. I apologize, Mrs. Meeks. With her, everything is about race."

"Miss Banner is correct Miss Nelson," Diana says. "Don't worry. These are the issues which I plan to address immediately. Overcrowding, proper funding, and keeping those test scores up through hard work and preparation is my top priority. I don't want to end up like the teachers in Atlanta," Diana vents.

"All I know is. The day I'm asked to throw on a hairnet and report to the cafeteria to serve lunch to those snotty nose kids is the day I quit," Miss Nelson jokes.

Everyone laughs.

"I don't think that it's going to come to that, Miss Nelson. I plan to take full advantage of the superintendent's open-door policy," Diana says.

Ruth and Miss Nelson pause and glance at one another. They both burst into laughter.

"What? Did I say something funny?" Diana asks.

"No offense, Mrs. Meeks, but the superintendent has one policy. "Those who play by his rules, get to play." Miss Nelson says.

Meanwhile, Arthur, unbeknownst to the women, is returning home from his interview. He enters the house carrying a couple of boxes of pizza. He inadvertently overhears their conversation.

"You just make sure you stay focused on the job young lady," Miss Nelson admonishes.

"I don't know what you mean," Diana replies.

"Oh, really?" She shoots her a suspicious stare down. "I mean, what was all that flirting we saw going on between you and Mr. Patterson yesterday?" Miss Nelson asks.

Stunned, Arthur stops in his tracks and continues listening.

"What! I don't know what you're talking about!" Diana shouts.

"So, are you telling me, that what Miss Banner and I saw yesterday, was all in our imagination? All that, 'Oh, Mr. Patterson, we need more men of God in the school system, was nothing, huh?"

Diana stands silent and stiff as she wants desperately to offer a defense against Miss Nelson's accusations. Ruth couldn't be more pleased by the potentially scandalous topic raised by Miss Nelson. With intense eagerness, she awaits Diana's response.

"Ok, maybe, I was a little over friendly, but I was just being polite. I was not flirting," Diana says.

Miss Nelson folds her arms and gives Diana an incredulous stare. Diana places her hand on her hip and stares back in defiance. After a few seconds, she can't continue the charade and folds under the pressure.

"Ok!" she shouts. "The man was fine! However, I was not flirting!"

"I knew it!" Miss Nelson yells.

They all laugh.

In the living room, Arthur grinds his teeth, and shakes his head in disbelief. He unbuttons his top shirt button to get some air. Mentally, he orders himself to calm down and relax. Seconds later, he enters the kitchen carrying the pizzas.

"Anybody hungry?" he asks. He annoyingly tosses the boxes on the kitchen counter.

Diana's eyes widen, and her voice becomes shaky.

"Hey, baby!" I didn't know you were here?" she replies.

"What? Did I miss something?" he asks.

Diana becomes giddy and she quickly changes the subject.

"Miss Banner; Miss Nelson, this is my husband Arthur.

"Please to meet you both." Arthur says.

"Hello, Arthur," Ruth responds.

"Hello, Arthur; we've heard so much about you," Miss Nelson says.

"Well, that's reassuring," Arthur says. He scans the room. "You all sure have done a great job."

"I could not have done it without these two," Diana says.

"Is that so?" He gives her a stern look. "Well, why don't you all treat yourselves to a little lunch?"

He opens the refrigerator and grabs a beer.

"A little early, isn't it?" Diana asks.

"Yes, it is," he snaps. "Is Caleb asleep?"

"Yes," Diana replies.

"Great!" He turns to Ruth and Miss Nelson. "If it's alright with you ladies, I'm going to take a moment to unwind, then I will pitch in."

Arthur takes his beer onto the patio. Arthur's behavior makes Diana concerned. Ruth, sensing the tension, and decides to seize the opportunity.

"If you both will excuse me, I think I'm going to have a smoke." She quickly grabs her cigarettes from the kitchen table and follows him outside.

On the patio, Arthur takes a seat in the patio chair. He hikes one leg up on the railing and turns up his beer. Ruth takes a seat next to him. She lights up and takes a drag.

"I'm sorry. I hope you don't mind the smoke," she says.

"No. I don't mind," he replies.

"She can be pretty demanding, huh?" she says.

"Yeah, well, she comes from a very demanding home. However, her bark is greater than her bite," he replies.

"I see. So, how are you enjoying Memphis so far?" she asks.

"We haven't seen much of it yet, but I can tell you, it's not Dallas. That's home."

"I must say, Arthur, I truly admire you," Ruth says. "I mean, moving away from your family and friends and with a new baby nevertheless."

"I took the vows," he replies.

"You know Arthur, my daddy ran his own school for close to thirty years. He would come home every day, and mother would have dinner prepared. After the family ate, he would retire to his study, smoke his cigar and have a glass of wine. You know what else, Arthur? My mother never nagged him about it either.

"Your father sounds like a lucky man," Arthur says.

"It wasn't luck. It was strength," Ruth replies.

She begins inappropriately rubbing his neck and back. Arthur's muscles tense. He gives her a nervous smile.

"You are a strong man, Arthur. In fact, you remind me of my father," she says. She seductively smiles at him. "Women respond to strong men."

Eager to be away from her, he gulps down the remainder of his beer, and then he places the bottle on the railing.

"I think I should get out of this suit and get in there and get to work," he says.

"Lead the way," Ruth replies.

Later that day, at the Health Center's Zumba class, Diana and Miss Nelson huddle at the water cooler, hydrating as they wait for the class to start.

"This looks like it's going to be lots of fun," Diana says.

"You might want to do some stretching," Miss Nelson replies. "Thirty minutes from now, it won't seem like much fun."

"You're probably right," Diana says.

The women find a secluded area in the gym and they begin stretching.

"Is this all one facility? It's huge," Diana says.

"It is. Let's see, they have a basketball court, a weight room, and they also have an indoor pool. I don't swim of course. I can't get the rhythm of the stroke," Miss Nelson jokes.

"You're crazy," Diana says. "Arthur would love it here. I think I'm going to surprise him with a family membership. I feel horrible leaving him alone with Caleb."

"You know, Mrs. Meeks, if you would like, I could give Aunt Jackie a call. I'm sure she wouldn't mind babysitting your son. She just loves children, and it would give Arthur and you some extra time alone if you know what I mean, "Miss Nelson says.

"I know exactly what you mean. Some alone time is long overdue," Diana replies. They laugh. "But, seriously, who is Aunt Jackie?" Diana asks.

"Listen to me," Miss Nelson replies. "I'm sorry. Jackie Miles is an old friend and colleague. To those of us close to her, she is Aunt Jackie. She quit teaching years ago to start a daycare. She is great with kids!"

"Really?"

"Unfortunately, though, she has had to scale back quite a bit since Joe, her husband passed away a few years ago. I worry about her sitting up in that big old house alone. I think she could really use the company."

"I see." Diana hesitates. "It's just that Caleb has never left our side since birth. But, then again, when Arthur starts to work, we will need someone to watch him. So, I guess it wouldn't be a bad idea to meet her," she says.

"Talk it over with Arthur, and let me know what you both decide," Miss Nelson replies. "I can arrange a meeting."

"I will. Thanks."

They continue stretching. Miss Nelson becomes concerned.

"Where on earth is Miss Banner?" she asks. "Class will be starting soon."

Just then, Diana spots Ruth entering the building. Her jaw drops.

"Not to worry, she made it," she says. She points at the entrance.

Miss Nelson is shocked to see Ruth standing there wearing a red headband, with matching wrist bands, a bright yellow tank top, crimson shorts, yellow leotards, and white glitter crafted gym shoes.

"What on earth?" she says.

Ruth approaches them.

"Hello, ladies."

"Hey there," Diana replies.

Looking up at her from the floor, Miss Nelson scans Ruth's outfit.

"Ruth, are you here for Zumba, or Woodstock?" she jokes.

Ignoring Miss Nelson's taunt, Ruth begins a series of stretches. Diana taps Miss Nelson on the leg, admonishing her for teasing. Miss Nelson chuckles.

Just then, a female voice blares over the loudspeaker. It is the first of two instructors preparing to get the Zumba class stated.

"Let's get ready to Zumba! AIAIAIAIAI!" she yells.

The participants scamper to the dance floor, and they evenly space their bodies apart from one another.

The second instructor dances about the room with a wireless headset microphone.

"We're about to have a Zumba party!" she shouts.

The class begins dancing in unison along with the music and following the directions of the instructor.

"Let's get sexy and burn some calories!" the first instructor shouts.

Everyone desperately tries to keep up. As instructor two makes her way across the room, she spots Diana, and she is impressed with her energy.

"Somebody's got the hang of it!" she says.

Her compliment of Diana makes Ruth jealous causing her to increase her energy. With clumsy adrenalin, Ruth invades the space of both Miss Nelson and Diana.

"Ruth! Really!" Miss Nelson complains.

Ruth's competitive zeal soon becomes too much for both women, and they surrender her more space. Instructor two makes her way back around the room to the area of Ruth.

"I like your energy!" she shouts.

Ruth smirks at Diana. Unsure of what to make of her behavior, Diana smiles nervously back at her.

Later, in the Health Center's female locker room after their shower, an exhausted Diana finishes getting dressed. Ruth is dressed and sitting on the bench packing her belongings. The women wait for

Miss Nelson to join them. Diana decides to engage Ruth on a pressing matter.

"Miss Banner, I need to ask you a question."

"Sure, what is it?" Ruth replies.

"The other night, Mr. Patterson phoned me. He said that you gave him my number?"

"That's correct. I didn't think you would mind."

"That's kind of what I wanted to speak with you about. I just wish you would have asked me first."

Ruth stops packing her bag.

"Oh, I'm sorry. I hope it didn't cause any concerns," she says.

"There is a part of my day that I like to set aside for family," Diana replies.

"You know, Mrs. Meeks, Dr. Lanier says, a principal's day doesn't end with the final bell."

Diana takes a deep breath, holds it in then releases.

"Kudos for Dr. Lanier, but I think it would have been more appropriate had you asked me first."

"Oh, I hope you can forgive me for being so, inappropriate." Ruth snaps back. She abruptly gabs her bag and storms off.

"That went well," Diana mumbles to herself.

Ruth bumps into Miss Nelson exiting the shower.

"Those were some smooth moves you showed us out there, Ruth!" she jokes.

Ruth ignores her and she continues walking. Miss Nelson approaches Diana.

"Is everything ok?"

"I think I just failed with my first diplomatic attempt to resolve an issue," Diana says.

Miss Nelson laughs.

"You'll get better at it. Miss Banner can be a real softy," Miss Nelson explains.

Meanwhile, in the ladies' room, Ruth tosses her gym bag onto the sink. She paces frantically mumbling to herself to calm her nerves.

"Keep it together, Ruth," she says.

She sighs, and then she suddenly stops and walks over to the mirror. She turns on the water, cups her hands and takes a palm full and splashes water on her face. She then calmly looks at her reflection in the mirror.

"You can handle this." she says to herself.

Minutes later, in the Health Center lobby a more tranquil Ruth rejoins Diana and Miss Nelson.

"Are we ready?" she asks.

"Are you ok, Ruth?" Miss Nelson responds.

"I'm fine."

They all head toward the exit. Not sure of what to make of Ruth's sudden change in behavior, Diana and Miss Nelson cautiously trail behind her.

In the parking lot, the women approach Ruth's vehicle, Ruth attempts to implement damage control. She stops walking and she turns to Diana. "I have an idea, Mrs. Meeks. Why don't you allow me to take you shopping this weekend? We can't have our new principal starting the new year in old clothes," she says.

A stunned Diana is speechless for a second, "No. Miss Banner, I can't let you do that."

"I insist."

"You can count me in," Miss Nelson interrupts.

"Alright then. See, Miss Nelson is in. What do you say?"

Miss Nelson nods her head, urging Diana to say yes.

Diana hesitates for a second.

"Fine, but only one outfit, and maybe a pair of shoes," she jokes.

"Alright!" Ruth yells. She opens her car door.

"I will call you later. Bye, now."

"Ok," Diana says. She turns to Miss Nelson. "I will let you know what Arthur and I decide about Aunt Jackie."

Ruth freezes in place.

"Jackie? What about Jackie?" she interrupts.

"Miss Nelson thought it might be a good idea for your friend to babysit my son."

Ruth quickly glances at Miss Nelson, who avoids eye contact with her.

Ruth turns to Diana. "Jackie and I are not friends," she snaps.

Ruth abruptly enters her vehicle, starts the engine and quickly drives off.

"Ok. What, exactly just happened?" Diana asks. "Walk with me. I should have warned you," Miss Nelson replies.

Miss Nelson enter locks her arm with Diana's arm and guides her in the direction of their vehicles.

"You should have warned me about what?" Diana asks.

"Jackie and Ruth haven't spoken in years."

"Why is that?"

"The details are sketchy, but one night, during a staff Christmas party, Joe, Jackie's' husband accused Ruth of making advances toward him, and Jackie didn't take it lying down. She and Ruth had a huge fight.

"Was it true?" Diana asks.

"Ruth vehemently denies it, but nevertheless, the situation caused a deep divide within our little clique," Miss Nelson replies. "The wounds are still very fresh with both women."

"No kidding.

As they reach their vehicles, they separate.

"Don't you worry. It's not your problem. You just might not want to mention Jackie's name much around Ruth," Miss Nelson says.

"Gotcha," Diana replies. "Hey, one other question."

"Sure. What's up?"

"How does she afford it? The lunch, the shopping I mean; and on a teacher's salary?" Diana asks.

"Oh, that. Ruth's father bought land in Mississippi when Ruth was young. When the casinos came, he leased a large portion of it to them. Ruth and her mother now share a trust fund."

"Must be nice."

"Yep, and while we are on the subject young lady, let me give you a little advice. When white people volunteer to spend some money on you, don't turn them down," Miss Nelson jokes.

Diana laughs. "You are so silly," she replies. "Bye." They enter their vehicles and drive away.

Later, at Ruth's home, a shirtless Carlos, surrounded by soda cans and food wrappings, is stretched out on the couch watching television.

Television narrator:

"Black people spend over one trillion dollars in this economy, sir, and have nothing to show for it."

Interviewer:

"So, what should be done in your mind to correct the problem?"

Carlos yells at the television in mockery of the men. "Who cares, man! Money, hoes, and clothes, that's what this shit is all about!"

Ruth enters the home, right in the middle of Carlos's rant. She tosses her gym bag on the floor in the corner and plumps down in the recliner. Carlos sits up, grabs the remote, and mutes the television.

"What the hell are you wearing?" he asks.

"What? It's my Zumba outfit?" she replies.

"Zooba!" he taunts. "That new principal got you running marathons and dressing in uniform now?"

"Zumba! You dope. For your information, she couldn't even keep up with me," she replies. Ruth removes her headband and tosses at him. "How is your car running?" she asks.

"She is running almost as fast as me. All she needs now is some bump."

He removes a car magazine from the coffee table and passes it to Ruth. The price tag of the stereo which Carlos has circled nearly knocks her out of her chair.

"Fifteen hundred dollars!" she shouts. She tosses the magazine on the table. "Why would anyone throw away money like that?"

"What's the big deal?" he replies. "Besides, if we were getting that principal pay, we could afford it. Oh, wait. I know what we can do," he says. - prodding her. "Maybe we should cut back on our jewelry purchases," he says.

Ruth appears confused by his statement.

"I thought you liked your class ring?" she asks. "I spent a lot of money on it."

"I wasn't talking about my ring," he replies. He gives her a suspicious stare down.

"I really don't need this right now," she says as she attempts to avoid his subtle accusation. "I'm going to take a shower. Could you clean up this mess?" I don't know how you plan to stay in shape eating like this all summer."

She stands, grabs her bag, and leaves the room.

"My speed is all natural," Carlos says. He leans back on the couch and props his feet up on the coffee table. "Besides, if I need to get in shape, I can come to the gym and do some Zooba with you," he taunts.

"It's Zumba!" she yells from the hallway.

Carlos sits silently for a few seconds, then, he mischievously glances over at the magazine lying on the coffee table.

In the bathroom shower, just as Ruth rinses the soap from her face, the shower curtain is abruptly snatched open.

"Carlos!" she yells.

A nude Carlos stands there. He grabs Ruth by her throat, and aggressively pulls her out of the shower. He begins passionately kissing her, while he ushers her into the adjourning bedroom. There, he shoves her wet body onto the bed. She screams out in ecstasy.

Shortly after, they cuddle under the sheets and Carlos slowly awakens and catches Ruth distracted in her own thoughts.

"What's on your mind?" he asks.

"I think I may have found something," she replies.

"Oh, yeah," he says. "What's her sin?" he asks.

"It's not her. It's the husband," she replies.

"Huh?

"He is weak, and we both know just what weak men like."

"Yes, we do," Carlos says. He begins intimately groping her.

"Stop it now. Get serious. I need you to be on stand-by, and ready with the camera when the time comes."

"I'm always ready."

At Aunt Jackie's house, the door flings open. Miss Nelson, along with Diana, and her family are standing on the porch. Jackie greets them with a loud yell.

"Bea! Get in here, girl! "She screams.

"Jackie!" Miss Nelson yells back. They hug. "It's So, good to see you!"

Everyone enters the house. Jackie steps back and admires the young couple.

"Is this our new principal?" she asks.

"It sure is," Miss Nelson replies. "Jackie Miles, meet Arthur and Diana Meeks. This little fellow here, is their son, Caleb."

Jackie removes the blanket from the baby's face to get a better look.

"Oh, he is adorable," she says.

"Pleased to meet you," Diana says. She extends her hand.

"No, ma'am," Jackie replies. "We give out hugs around here." She hugs Diana and Arthur, then steps back and takes a second look at her. "You were right, Bea. They are making them younger."

Slightly irritated, Diana side-eyes Miss Nelson, but attempts to maintain a positive demeanor. Caleb becomes excited by Jackie's presence. Everyone is surprised when he attempts to communicate with her.

"I told you Mrs. Meeks. Kids really love Aunt Jackie," Miss Nelson says.

"You weren't kidding. I have never seen him respond to anyone like that," Diana replies.

"That's because there is only one Aunt Jackie," Jackie interrupts. She takes Caleb from Arthur. "Let's go down to the den. I have a play-pen with your name on it, little man," she says.

As everyone makes themselves comfortable on the sofa, Jackie returns with a tray of cookies and a pitcher of iced tea. Caleb enjoys himself playing with the toys Aunt Jackie placed in his play-pen. She places the tray on the table, then takes a seat next to the couple. Everyone helps themselves to cookies.

"You have a lovely home," Diana says.

"Thank you," she replies. "Joe and I bought this house when we first got married. That was a long time ago,"

"It's huge. I'll be glad when we can afford a home like this," Diana says.

"We will, baby, in time," Arthur replies. He can't help but feel the indirect pressure from her statement.

"Listen to your husband, Diana. A house can be a lot of work. In fact, I have been thinking about selling and moving into one of those new condos downtown," Jackie says.

"Now, Jackie, what are you going to do in a condo? Those are for young people," Miss Nelson replies.

"I beg your pardon. There is still a little fire left in this oven. Which, reminds me."

Jackie stands and walks over to the bookshelf. She retrieves a yearbook.

"What are you up to now?" Miss Nelson asks.

"I thought Mrs. Meeks would like to see what real divas we were back in the day," Jackie responds. Returning to her chair, she opens the book. Miss Nelson squeals with embarrassment.

"Oh, my Lord!" she shouts. "Why do you even have this? Don't you have any more modern photos?" she asks.

"I do, but you're not as shapely in those," Jackie taunts.   "We sure had some good times though. "Didn't we, Bea?"

"We sure did."

"Are those stone-washed jeans, Miss Nelson?" Arthur mocks.

"Uh, as a matter of fact they are, and I was rocking them too," she replies.

"Arthur, Bea's physique was the envy of all the women on staff back then," Jackie says.

"Excuse me!" Miss Nelson shouts.

"Miss Banner sure looks nice," Diana interrupts.

"Huh, how is the trollop these days?" Jackie responds.   "You better watch your husband Diana. Now that she has lost all that weight, no man is safe in her presence."

"Jackie, Really?" Miss Nelson shouts.

Jackie chuckles.

"Alight, I'll be good.   She points to a photo of coach.   "Boy, Coach Curry sure was a looker.   Are you still sweet on him, Bea?" Jackie asks.

Stunned by her candor, Miss Nelson gives Jackie a stern stare. Jackie laughs and playfully slaps her on the knee.

"Did I say something wrong?" she asks.

"For the record, he was sweet on me," Miss Nelson replies.

"Oh, that's right. I forgot," Jackie says.

"Dr. Lanier is handsome," Diana says.

"Speaking of Dr. Lanier Jackie, maybe you can tell us where we can find him?" Miss Nelson asks.

"Oh. Uh, left for vacation... the Bahamas, I think."

Jackie suddenly disengages from the conversation. Her trembling hands take possession of the yearbook. Miss Nelson squints at her sudden odd behavior. Jackie stands and returns the book to the shelf and then returns to her chair. She quickly changes the conversation.

"Alright, so, tell me about this babysitting idea," she says.

At that moment, Diana's phone rings.

"Sorry, give me just a second. Hello."

Everyone waits patiently. Miss Nelson locks her eyes in on Jackie. She is still suspicious as to why Jackie appears to seem so nervous. Jackie avoids eye contact with her.

"Hello, Mrs. Meeks."

"Miss Banner, could I get back with you. I'm in the middle of something," Diana says.

Jackie makes a cruel comment and laughs. Ruth overhears her and interrogates Diana.

"Are you at Jackie's house?" she asks.

"Yes, as a matter of fact, I am," Diana replies. "I'll call you when I'm done here."

Diana hangs up. Ruth becomes enraged and she slams the phone down.

"So, like I was saying. We were hoping maybe you could help us out and watch him from time to time, or just until we get settled and find a permanent daycare."

Caleb squeals with excitement from the playpen.

"It seems as though Caleb has made up his mind," Arthur Jokes

Everyone laughs.

"Well, I sure have made up mine," Jackie replies. "It can be pretty lonely around here. I could stand having a man around the house."

"If it's not too much trouble, Jackie, we were kind of hoping we could bring him by tomorrow," Arthur interrupts.

"Tomorrow?" Jackie replies.

Diana is caught off guard and a little embarrassed by his request.

"When did we decide this?" she asks.

"I'm sorry, baby. I should have said something earlier," he replies. "I was thinking we could get out and do a little sightseeing."

"I wish you had said something," Diana replies.

Keenly aware of Diana's displeasure with Arthur's request, Jackie comes to his rescue.

"Tomorrow, it will be just fine," she says. She walks over and lifts Caleb from the playpen. "We are going to have a good time, aren't we, little man?"

Later, on the porch,

"Bye." Jackie yells as she stands watching as the group walk down her walkway to their vehicles.

"I will call you later, Jackie," Miss Nelson responds.

Arthur secures Caleb in his baby seat. Diana opens the passenger side-door. She stops and turns to Miss Nelson.

"Hey, what are you doing tonight?" she asks.

"No plans. Why?"

"Arthur has a fight party. I was thinking we could have a girl's night."

"I like that plan," Miss Nelson says. "I can be there around seven."

"That's fantastic. I'll see you then."

The couple enters their vehicle and then drives away.

Later that evening, at Arthur and Diana's home, Arthur prepares to leave. With Caleb in her arms, Diana walks him to the door.

"I won't stay out too late," he says.

"Stay as long as you like. We'll be fine," Diana replies. She kisses him.

Just as Arthur opens the door, Miss Nelson arrives.

"Hey, you," he says.

"Hello, Arthur," she greets him.

"I'm headed out. Could you try not to get my wife too drunk?" he jokes.

"I'm not making any promises," she responds.

Arthur laughs.

"See you guys in a bit."

"Bye, babe." Diana closes the door behind him. "Come with me. I think I just about got him to sleep."

Miss Nelson follows her to the couple's bedroom. Diana places Caleb in his crib. Miss Nelson sits at the edge of the bed and observes the tidiness of the room.

"The place is really looking good Mrs. Meeks."

"Thank you. I could never have done it without you guys." "Thanks again."

"You're welcome."

Miss Nelson spots the couple's wedding photo on the dresser. With a coveting gaze upon that drifts to envy, she sulks.

"You really are a blessed woman, Mrs. Meeks," she says.

Diana turns and notices Miss Nelson's attention glued to her wedding photo.

"Oh, yeah, that," Diana replies.

Miss Nelson is taken back by her response. She pats the bed; beckoning Diana to sit beside her.

"You know, when you invited me over tonight, I suspected that it wasn't just for drinks and small talk. What's on your mind?" she asks.

"Please don't judge me," Diana replies.

"I wouldn't do that. So, what's wrong?

Diana pauses for a second.

"You ever feel like you are moving in the right direction, or, at least, the direction everyone says you should be moving, but nothing feels, right?" Diana asks.

"Every day, but could you be more specific?" Miss Nelson replies.

"What I'm trying to say is, I got my dream job. I have a loving husband, and a son whom I adore."

"So, what's the problem?" Miss Nelson asks.

"It's just that sometimes it all can get overwhelming. Do you know what I mean? It's like I can't make everyone happy. My mother-"

"Your mother; tell me about your mother?"

"Well, she wasn't exactly thrilled when I decided to marry Arthur, and she was even less enthused when I got pregnant. She thought I needed to enjoy being single for a while longer."

"And how do you feel?" Miss Nelson asks.

"That's just what I mean. Some days, I'm not sure," Diana replies.

"Miss Meeks, do you love your husband?" Miss Nelson asks.

"Of course, I do," Diana quickly replies.

"Then, you have your answer. Diana, listen to me. There is not a single person on this planet who at some point have not questioned their major decisions. God knows I have."

Still unconvinced, Diana sulks. Miss Nelson lifts Diana's chin.

"You have got to have faith. He doesn't put more on us than we can handle. Do you understand?"

Diana smiles, and she nods her head in agreement.

"I do." The two of them embrace.

"As far your mother goes, trust me. She will come around," Miss Nelson says.

"Thank you, and thanks for coming over," Diana replies.

"You are welcome. If you ever need to talk about anything, I will be here to listen.

Diana pauses for a second, as she searches for the right words.

"Do you mind if I ask you a personal question?" she asks.

"Wow, that was fast, but go ahead."

"What exactly did happen between you and Coach?" she asks.

Stunned by her candor Miss Nelson's eyes widen, and she takes a deep breath.

"When he was in love with me, I was not ready to be married. He married someone else. He divorced and married someone younger. That's the meat of the story," she replies.

"Sorry. I didn't mean to pry," Diana says as she senses Miss Nelson has become uncomfortable with the subject.

Miss Nelson chuckles.

"Oh, it's ok, "Miss Nelson replies. "I'll say one thing for sure, you got me ready for my drink now.

I'm just up here confessing like I'm in catholic school." They both laugh.

"Alright. Let's do it! to the den." Diana shouts. "I'm right behind you." Miss Nelson replies. "Diana pauses "Oh, wait. "I should call Miss Baxter and let her know that I can't go shopping tomorrow."

Diana grabs her phone from the nightstand and begins dialing.

Meanwhile, at Ruth's home, Carlos relaxes on the couch watching television. Lying next to him is Ruth's cell phone. With his eyes glued to the screen, he reaches for it. He takes a glance at the phone display, and notices that the call is from Diana. He quickly presses the ignore button.

"Huh, that's strange. I think she ignored my call." Diana says.

"Don't worry about it. I will let her know you and Arthur made other plans when I meet her tomorrow. When she gets herself a man, she will understand," Miss Meeks Jokes.

"That is not a nice thing to say. I just don't want another episode," Diana says.

"I know how to handle Ruth. Now, stop stalling. I need my drink," Miss Nelson replies.

They excitingly exit the bedroom.

The following day, Arthur and Diana tour Memphis. Their adventurous outing includes visits to the Stax Museum, the Civil Rights Museum, and world-famous Beale Street, which is where they stop for lunch.

On the restaurant balcony, Diana scans through a tourist brochure. Arthur places a dollar bill in a pale carried by one young man collecting money for his friends as they turn somersaults down the middle of Beale Street.

"I think we should visit the Pink Palace, or maybe the Zoo after lunch. Which do you think?" Diana asks.

"Slow down, baby. We don't have to see it all in one day. This is our home now," he replies.

"Sorry. You're right."

Sensing that now would be a good time to have a conversation, Arthur reaches for Diana's hand, and began struggling for words.

"Honey," he says. "I want to ask you a question."

Concerned by his sudden mood change, Diana drops the brochure, surrenders her hand and gives him her full attention. "What's wrong?"

"Are you happy?" he asks.

"Why would you ask me that? Of course, I'm happy."

"It's just that —" Diana's phone rings, breaking her attention. Arthur becomes annoyed by the interruption. She removes her hand from Arthur's grasp, grabs her phone and glances at the display.

"Oh, God! What now?" she mumbles.

"What is it?" Arthur asks.

Diana cuts him off by holding up a finger. She answers the phone. Arthur's frustration heightens.

"Miss Banner, how can I help you now?" she asks.

"Hello, Mrs. Meeks. I hope I didn't catch you at an inappropriate time," Ruth taunts. "I just thought you might want to know what a great time Miss Nelson and I had today."

"I'm glad to hear it. I wish I could have joined you," Diana replies.

"You know, Missy, when I agreed to this whole mentoring idea, it wasn't because I didn't have anything else better to do with my time," Ruth snaps.

"I assure you that thought never entered my mind," Diana replies. "Did you just call me Missy?"

"Good, because I would hate to think that your parents raised such a rude child."

"Excuse me! I did try reaching out to let you know my plans changed. I was also under the impression that Miss Nelson explained things to you. I apologize for the misunderstanding."

"She did explain, but I didn't think it was her responsibility to do so. If I recall, you were the one I invited, not her. Communication is an essential part of becoming an effective administrator young lady."

"Ok, I'm going to end this call, before I say

something that destroys any chance of us having a productive relationship. Good-bye!"

"I'm not finished! I —" Ruth yells.

Diana abruptly ends the call before hearing another word. She slams the phone down on the table.

"Are you ok?" Arthur asks.

Her flaring nostrils and protruding eyes prevent him from probing any further.

Meanwhile, at Ruth's home, she storms into the living room. She screams out in anger, startling Carlos.

"What is it!" he replies.

Ignoring him, she paces the room, and takes hard uncontrolled breaths. Then she suddenly stops. With a deep sense of clarity, she stares directly at Carlos. Without uttering a word, Carlos can read her energy loud and clear.

"Yeah, it's about time," he says.

A few days later, Carlos cruises South Memphis. As he bounces his head to the sounds of his new car stereo, he pulls in front of an apartment building. Sitting outside of one of the complexes is his young cousin Leslie, and her friend Mercedes. Leslie is braiding Mercedes's hair. The thump of Carlos's stereo grabs Leslie's attention.

"What's up, cuz!" she shouts to him.

"What it do!" he yells back.

Suddenly, emerging from inside the apartment is his very scantily dressed, and shapely older cousin, Passion. She walks swiftly past the girls and heads toward the car.

"I ain't bailing yo ass out of jail!" Leslie yells out to her.

Without tuning to acknowledge her, Passion holds up a vulgar finger gesture. As she reaches the sidewalk, three young boys on bicycles take shade beneath a tree nearby.

"Hey, Passion baby... when you gone get with me," one young man taunts.

"When you get some money, and a real mode of transportation," Passion snaps back.

She opens the passenger-side door and enters the car. The other boys tease the young man, as Carlos and Passion drive away.

Back on the on the porch, "Yo cousin a G?" Mercedes asks.

"Girl, naw," Leslie replies. "That nigga ain't no gangster. His folks live out East. He a Cordova thug."

"He go to Riverside. Right?" Mercedes asks.

"That's because he stay with my uncle during the school year," she replies.

"For real? Well, gangster or not, I'll still hit that," Mercedes says.

"Uhg!" Leslie replies as she adjusts Mercedes's head. "Stop talking nasty about my folks and hold your head still."

Later, in the Health Center parking lot, Passion and Carlos sit inside Carlos's vehicle and take a final moment to tie up loose ends. Carlos pulls out of his wallet Diana's family photo. He reveals the picture to Passion.

"That's him," he says.

"You got my money, right?" Passion asks.

"You will get your money. You just stick to the plan. Let's go."

The two of them exit the vehicle and head toward the entrance.

Inside the gym, Carlos spots Arthur. He points to Passion of Arthur's location. The two split up. Passion begins walking seductively over to Arthur while catching the eye of every man inside of the facility.

"Hello," she says as she reaches him. "I'm Teresa, but my friends call me Passion."

"Oh, hello," Arthur replies. He is stunned by her beauty. "I'm Arthur; please to meet you."

"Are you new here, Arthur?" she asks.

"Yes," he replies. "My wife and I recently moved here." He becomes embarrassed because of her confused stare. "Oh, I'm sorry; you meant here, at the gym."

Passion is amused by Arthur's nervous behavior.

"Yes, silly. I meant here at the gym. So, you're married?" she asks.

"Yes," he quickly responds.

Passion quickly scans the gym for Carlos's whereabouts. Once she spots him on second floor, he gives her a thumbs up, and she jumps into character. She seductively struts behind Arthur and places her hands on his shoulders.

"You know Arthur, I have always wanted someone to show me how to bench press. Do you mind?"

"Well, I — "

"Pleeese, she whines." "I promise not to get in your way."

Arthur hesitates for a second, then finally concedes.

"Sure. Why not?" he says.

"Yippee!".

On the second floor, Carlos slips into a small utility closet. Just as he removes his camera from his bag, a gym maintenance worker opens the door.

"Excuse me sir. Is there something I can help you with?" he asks.

Carlos nervously fumbles with the equipment. "Oh, my bad," he replies. He quickly places the camera back inside the bag. "I was just checking my equipment."

"I'm afraid I'm going to have to ask you to do that somewhere else."

Visibly irritated, Carlos snatches his bag and exits the closet.

"Alright! I'm leaving," he snaps.

He zips his bag and heads back downstairs.

As he frantically searches for a new hiding place, Suddenly, Jay, a member of the Riverside track-team, spots him, "Hey, Los, come holla at your boy mane!" Jay yells.

Jay's outburst draws the attention of Arthur and Passion. Carlos's eyes widen. He gives a tentative smile and a quick head jerk. He walks over to greet Jay. Arthur notices the Riverside gym bag he is carrying.

"What's up. fool?" Jay says. They shake hands. "I'm here trying to get like you. We got to take state again next year. You feel me?"

"Yeah, no doubt," Carlos replies.

Arthur spots Passion's final rep on the free weight, then interrupts the boy's conversation as Passion nervously looks on.

"Excuse me. Are you fellows' students at Riverside?" he asks.

"That's right," Jay replies.

"I'm Arthur Meeks. My wife is going to be your new principal."

"Oh snap, that's what's up. I'm Jay. This is the team's superstar and my main my man, Los."

Jay gives Arthur a hip handshake. Arthur tries to keep up but doesn't quite get it. Carlos gives Arthur a normal handshake.

"Oh, ok. Pleased to meet you both. So, what sport do you guys play?"

"We're on the track team," Jay says. "My man Los was all-state two years in a row."

"Is that so?" Arthur responds.

"A little something," Carlos says.

"Ah, fool, stop being modest," Jay replies.

"That's quite an accomplishment, Carlos. You should be proud. I ran track in college." Arthur says.

"Yeah, what event?" Jay asks.

"I ran the forty."

"Dude…" He nudges Carlos. "That's what you run. What's your best time?" Jay asks.

"Well, I don't want to brag, but I ran a four-three actually," Arthur replies.

"Whoa!" Jay shouts.

"That's what's up," Carlos says.

"You two should race for real," Jay instigates.

Arthur laughs.

"I don't know. I may not be able to keep up with you younger guys," Arthur says.

"Hello. Are we done? "an impatient Passion interrupts.

"Oh, I'm sorry," Arthur says. "I lost focus. Well, good luck to the both of you. I hope I get to catch a few meets this year."

"That's cool. I got to get out of here," Carlos says. "I'll catch you later, Jay."

"Later, fool," Jay replies.

As Carlos walks away, Arthur notices his camera lens is poking through the top of his bag.

"Hey, Carlos, don't lose your camera. It looks expensive," Arthur shouts.

Carlos turns, and gives Arthur a glazed stare. Arthur points to the bag. Carlos looks down, to notice that his gym bag was not zipped properly, and his camera lens is exposed.

"Oh, shit," he mumbles. He quickly shoves the camera inside. "I got it. Thanks."

He makes a beeline for the exit.

In the gym parking lot, Carlos waits anxiously inside his vehicle. A short while later, Passion exits the building, and hurries to the car. She enters the vehicle.

"So, did you get them?" she asks.

"No."

"What happened?"

"I couldn't get in position."

"Why did you leave? I could have kept his attention all day. He was feeling' me," she says.

"He saw me, and he saw the camera. I can't send pictures from inside the gym. Don't you think they gone suspect something?" he asks.

"Huh, I guess." She pauses. "Well, where my money at?"

"Money? money, for what!"

"How bout for starters, my time, this outfit, and me getting my hair did. Which I did all for this little failed mission impossible, Tom Cruise!"

Carlos's face tightens with frustration. As he removes his wallet from his back pocket. He opens it, exposing two $100 bills. He removes one of them and hands it to her.

"Here, mane!" he snaps at her.

Passion takes the money and stashes it inside her bosom.

"Thank you. Now, I need you to take me to the club. This ass might as well make some real money since I'm dressed for it," she says.

"Whatever," he angrily replies.

Carlos starts up the engine and then speeds out of the parking lot.

A short while later, Carlos pulls up to the gentlemen's Club. Passion exits the vehicle, closes the door, then leans inside the window.

"Thanks, cuz. We should do this again soon," she sarcastically says.

She smiles, turns, and walks away. Carlos lustfully stares at her ass as she walks away. Unexpectedly, she turns and catches him.

"Ugh, really?" she yells.

Carlos gives a mischievous grin, then drives away.

In Ruth's bedroom, Carlos stands at the dresser unpacking the camera and supplies from the gym bag. A very irritated Ruth pace behind him.

"What went wrong?" she asks. "I thought you said you had everything under control."

"I got compromised, alright."

"Do you even know what that word means?"

She places her hands on her forehead in distress and looks up at the ceiling. Carlos shoves the gym bag and camera, causing some items on the dresser to tumble over.

"Look, he noticed me before I could get any shots!" he shouts.

"Could you please not break the camera?" Ruth admonishes.

"Ain't nobody gone break this camera!"

Ruth moves about, unable to settle her nerves. She rubs the back of her neck to relieve tension, pondering what to do next.

"I think I got an idea. I'm going to need you to be ready with the camera when I call. Can I at least count on you for that?" she asks.

"I got this," he insists.

"Yeah, sure," she says. "Give me the money?"

"I don't have it. I had to pay Passion.

"Why on earth would you pay her two hundred dollars, when she obviously didn't do anything to earn it?" Ruth asks.

"She did what I asked her to do. So, she deserved to get paid. That's the way business works," he naively explains.

"Well, I guess when you're doing business with other people's money, you can afford to take some losses. Is that it, Carlos?"

Ruth aggressively engages him while waving her finger at his face. "Answer me! Is that it!" Unable to endure the onslaught any longer, he grabs her around the neck and squeezes until she becomes short of breath and paralyzed with fear.

"Let's get something straight. Your money is my money. You understand?"

"Yes," Ruth, terrified for life, faintly whispers.

Carlos slowly releases pressure and turns her lose. He turns his back to her and begins reorganizing the items on the dresser he'd previously knocked over. Ruth stands there visibly shaken. Carlos, with his head lowered and eyes raised, watches Ruth's reflection through the dresser mirror.

"Put some steaks on the grill. A nigga hungry," he commands.

Ruth immediately rushes from the bedroom and into the hallway. There, she backs against the wall, still trembling with fear from the ordeal and weeps silently.

134

****

The next day at Arthur and Diana's home, Diana casually moves about the kitchen preparing the family dinner. She grabs a bowl and begins stirring her cornbread mix. The house phone rings. Annoyed by the inconvenience, she sighs heavily, then stops mixing and grabs the phone from its base.

"Hello!"

"Hello, Mrs. Meeks, I hope I did not catch you at a bad time."

"Oh, it's you. I'm in the middle of preparing dinner."

"Great. Well, I won't keep you. How is the family?" Ruth asks.

"Everyone is fine," an annoyed Diana snaps at her. She rolls her eyes in frustration. "Is there something important on your mind?"

"I just want to apologize about the other day. I was completely out of line."

"Yeah, well, unfortunately, it's becoming a habit."

"I should not have spoken to you in the way."

"Fine; apology accepted. Is that it?" Diana asks.

"I was hoping I could maybe treat you to lunch; just you and me. I really would like for us to remain friends," Ruth says.

Diana goes silent, momentarily disengaged from the conversation. As much as she would love to really give Ruth a piece of her mind, she realizes that she still must maintain a civil rapport with everyone on staff at Riverside. She is the new kid on the block, and besides, how would Dr. Lanier and the superintendent view her ability to run the school if she can't resolve a personal issue between a fellow colleague.

"Ok, but look, I don't want--- "

"Great, Ruth interrupts." "How's this Tuesday? I'll text you the time and place. Bye, now."

Ruth abruptly ends the call. Diana stands there stunned by her abrasive behavior. She shakes her head.

"This woman is crazy," she mumbles.

The next day at the Harbor Town Market, Mr. Patterson casually strolls along the meat aisle, pushing his basket and talking on his cell phone.

"I wish I knew. Communication is the most important part of any relationship. I happen to recall a certain someone once told me that."

Ruth suddenly appears from the adjoining aisle pushing an empty cart. She positions her basket in front of his, blocking his forward progress. Mr. Patterson's eyes widen, and for a second, he mentally breaks from his phone conversation. Ruth smiles at him. He nervously nods, acknowledging her and somewhat taken back by her odd behavior.

"Can I call you later?" he says to the caller on the phone. A deep male voice can be heard on the other end. *"Yes. Let's talk soon."* He ends the call. "Miss Banner, I didn't know you shopped here."

"Hello, Mr. Patterson. It is a nice surprise running into you," Ruth says.

"I live nearby. Sundays are my shopping day," he replies.

"I know," she says.

"Pardon me? How did you know?" He asks.

Ruth ignores him and quickly changes the subject.

"So, how are budget talks going with Mrs. Meeks?" she asks.

"Yeah, about that, I think talks may have stalled right out of the gate."

"Are you sure about that? She has had nothing but good things to say about you. I think she has a soft spot for Ministers."

"Really?"

"Oh, yes sir, and she's always going on about how she feels it's important to build strong relationships with members of the faculty."

"She certainly sounds ambitious. Maybe I should reach out to her again?"

"You know what, I am having lunch with her on Tuesday. You should join us. As head of the English department, you might want to get a jump start, building your strong relationship with her," Ruth suggests.

He mulls over the suggestion for a few seconds.

"Well, I suppose. I'm not doing anything Tuesday."

"Great! Remember. We will be meeting Tuesday at noon at The Red Apple Lounge. See you there," Ruth confirms cheerfully.

She then quickly turns with her basket and hurries off down the aisle before he can respond.

"Ok." He stands there confused by her sudden dismissal. "It was nice talking to you," he mumbles.

Tuesday, at the Red Apple Lounge, Diana waits alone at the table, repeatedly glancing at her watch. Suddenly, Mr. Patterson approaches her.

"Good afternoon, Mrs. Meeks," he says.

"Mr. Patterson; hello."

He points to an empty chair.

"May I?" he asks.

"Please do. "she replies. "I'm just waiting for Miss Banner. Guess she is running a little behind."

"Good. That gives me time to make a better first impression," he says.

"I don't recall your first impression being all that bad," she replies.

"So, you didn't mind the late-night phone call?"

"Oh, that. Now, that was a bad second impression. Our first meeting was at the school. Remember?

They both laugh.

"Ok, you got me," he says.

The waitress arrives at the table.

"What can I get you to drink?" she asks.

"I will have a Long Island Iced Tea," Mr. Patterson responds. Diana is shocked.

"Mr. Patterson, I thought you were a man of the cloth?"

"I am, but Jesus did turn water to wine. Who's to say He didn't have a glass himself?" he jokes.

"If that is the case, I'll have what he is having."

The waitress smiles and walks away. Mr. Patterson notices Diana nervously twisting her wedding ring.

"I hope I didn't cause any confusion the other night."

"What?" she asks. She then notices him watching her fidget with her ring. "Oh, no. not at all; Arthur is very understanding. In fact, I sometimes wonder how I got so lucky."

"Well, I would say, he is a pretty lucky fellow as well," he replies.

Diana blushes and quickly takes a sip of water. The waitress returns with the drinks.

Across the street from the Restaurant, Carlos is sitting in his car. He aims his camera and then snaps several pictures of Diana and Mr. Patterson as they engage in conversation.

Inside the restaurant, Mr. Patterson holds up his glass for a toast. "Here is to new beginnings," he says.

"To new beginnings," Diana replies. The two of them touch glasses.

Outside, Carlos smiles. "That's right love birds. Live it up, "he mumbles. He snaps a few more shots, then lowers his camera and drives away.

Two days later, at Arthur and Diana's home, a visibly angry Arthur sits on the edge of the couple's bed, as he anxiously anticipates Diana's return home. Caleb is asleep in his crib. A bubbly Diana enters the bedroom.

"Hey! How are my two favorite men?" she asks.

"You mind explaining these," Arthur snaps. He tosses the photos across the bed to her.

She retrieves them.

"What's this?" she replies. "Have you been spying on me?"

Arthur becomes livid by her accusation. He jumps from the bed.

"Spying on you?" he shouts. "No. I haven't been spying on you, but maybe I should have been less trusting. I thought you were having lunch with Miss Banner."

Arthur grabs his keys and bolts past her.

"Arthur, wait!"

He abruptly stops.

"No! You wait! I don't know what hurts the most. Your lying, or the fact that you seem to think you're the only one of us making real sacrifices to be here! "

"Arthur! I can explain!"

"Save it, Diana! I don't know if I made the right decision to come here."

"What are you saying?"

"You heard me! Look. I'm tired of pretending that everything is ok. I agreed to move here because I thought I was doing the right thing; being the supportive husband and all that, but you don't give a damn about any of my sacrifices. It's all about what you want! You constantly ignore me every time I attempt to communicate with you. You got me lying to the neighbors, because you were too selfish to go to a fight party, and now this!"

"Is that what this is about? You are mad because I wouldn't go to a fight party with you?" she asks.

"Jesus!" he shouts. "You just don't get it! The point is, I've been here for you; for everything you've asked me to do. You have done nothing to show me that you are here for me. Oh, yeah. About the other day, I did overhear you gloat on how fine you thought Mr. Patterson was."

"That was just girl talk," Diana says.

"Well, at least, you're talking to somebody." He replies. He storms out.

Diana slumps down on the bed shaking her head as she examines the photographs.

Later, at Aunt Jackie's house, the phone rings. "Hello. Oh, hi Diana, what's up?"

"Hi, Jackie." Her voice trembles. "I hate to bother you," Diana says.

"Diana, what's wrong?" Jackie asks.

"It's Arthur," Diana says.

"Has something happened to Arthur?" Jackie asks.

"We had a fight, and he stormed out. I have been trying to reach him, but he won't answer his cell."

"Oh no. What were you two fighting about?"

"All I know is, when I got home, he had these pictures."

"Pictures, what kind of pictures?" Jackie asks.

"Just some photos, with me having lunch with Mr. Patterson, I can't really explain everything right now," Diana replies.

"Where did he get them? Did he say?"

"No. He didn't, but they are really not that important. I was hoping you could watch Caleb for me while I track Arthur down and talk some sense into him."

Jackie pauses for a second.

"Diana, I want you to listen to me carefully. I want you to come over to my house, and bring those photos," Jackie says.

"Why? What's wrong, Jackie, and what are you not telling me?"

"Just do as I ask, please, I'll explain when you get here."

Aunt Jackie hangs up the phone. She sighs heavily and takes a seat in her recliner. She pauses for a second to think, and then she begins dialing. A man's voice answers on the other end.

"Hello."

"We have a problem," Jackie sternly says.

Later, at Jackie's home, the door opens, and with a big smile, she warmly invites Diana inside. Diana, cuddling Caleb, cautiously enters.

"Everyone is down in the den," Jackie says.

"Everyone?" Diana asks.

"You go on in," Jackie replies. She takes Caleb. "I'll be there shortly. I'm going to lay him down."

Diana finds herself standing alone in the hallway. She slowly walks down the hall, toward the den. As she turns the corner and enters the room, she spots two familiar faces sitting together on the sofa.

"Dr. Lanier, Mr. Patterson what are you doing here?" she asks.

The men stand. "Hello, Mrs. Meeks," Dr. Lanier responds.

"Good afternoon, Mrs. Meeks," Mr. Patterson replies.

Aunt Jackie enters. A confused Diana probes her.

"What's going on, Jackie?"

"I think I can help answer that," Dr. Lanier interrupts. "Let me first start by apologizing to you, Miss Meeks.

"Why? I don't understand," Diana says.

"First, I must apologize for disappearing on you the way I did." "Secondly," he hesitates, then sighs. "I haven't been completely honest with you as to why I recruited you."

"What are you saying, Dr. Lanier? Will someone please just tell me what's going on?"

"Why don't we all have a seat," Dr. Lanier says.

Everyone sits. Dr. Lanier opens his briefcase and pulls out a manila envelope. He passes it to Diana. A bewildered Mr. Patterson looks on.

"It seems as though you are not the only photogenic person in the room, Mrs. Meeks," he says. "I too have an admirer."

Diana cautiously removes the photographs from the package. She yelps and gasps at first glance. Both horrified, and speechless she can't believe her own eyes. She slowly passes the pictures back to him. Mr. Patterson quickly snatches the photos from Dr. Lanier's hands. The pictures expose the secret that they both believed that only they shared. The photos revealed several shots of Mr. Patterson and Dr. Lanier kissing in a hotel parking lot.

"How long have you had these!" Mr. Patterson yells. "When were you going to tell me about them?"

"Calm down James, please. About six months ago, someone placed them on my windshield," Dr. Lanier replies. "They also left a message recommending that I retire, or risk being outed."

"But you're married?" Diana interrupts.

"Yes. About that, Celeste and I are separating," Dr. Lanier replies. He turns back to Mr. Patterson. "This is why I left. She and I needed time away together to discuss things."

"I'm so sorry, William," Jackie says.

"You knew?" Diana asks.

"Yes. I've always known," Jackie replies.

"I don't expect you to fully understand it all, Mrs. Meeks," Dr. Lanier says. "This is something I have struggled with for most of my life. When I met James, he was much like you. He was a young, bright and passionate teacher. I became his mentor, and well,

"And we fell in love," Mr. Patterson interrupts.

"What I want to know is, why did you keep this from me? I would have understood."

"I felt the best thing was for me to handle it myself," Dr. Lanier replies. "I had Riverside to consider. If I retired, then it all goes away. However, it appears I was wrong. When Jackie explained that you had become a target Mr. Meeks, I had to come clean."

Diana closes her eyes and rubs the middle of her forehead, as she tries to make sense of it all.

"Ok, so, you are married, you are both gay, and you are being framed. I got that, but why am I a target? Are you telling me that you selected me to cover all of this up?" Diana asks.

"That's absolutely not the case." Dr. Lanier responds. "I chose you because Riverside needed you." He pauses, then grabs her hand. "And because you were an outsider. You were someone with no connection to the school. I didn't know who I could trust, and my suspicion has been confirmed. It is obvious now, that someone close to Riverside is responsible for all of this."

"Why didn't you contact the police?" Mr. Patterson asks.

"Look, the way I saw it, I was going to retire in a few years anyway, and let's be honest, I haven't exactly been doing a very good job these last few years," Dr. Lanier replies. "I doubt Principal Jackson would be pleased by the direction the school is headed."

"So, the bottom line is, we still don't know who is behind this," Diana says.

"Huh, I know who it is. It's Rachel Dolezal," Jackie replies.

"Who!" Everyone shouts in unison.

"Doesn't anyone watch the news? The white girl or whichever from the N.A.A.C.P; she pretended to be black. Never mind. What I'm trying to say is AKA, Ruth Banner!" Jackie replies.

"Miss Banner?" Diana asks.

"For God's sake, Jackie!" Dr. Lanier yells. "You want everyone to believe that Miss Banner has been running around, jumping over fences and hiding behind bushes just to set me up?"

"Look, I don't know how she did it or why, but trust me. She is involved somehow," Jackie insists.

"Give me a break," Dr. Lanier responds.

"You know, I love you William, but if you want to hear the truth, you are partly to blame for all of this," Jackie says.

"Me!" he shouts back.

"Yes! You!" Jackie yells. "That woman has always been a lying, spoiled sex addicted lunatic for as long as we have known her, but for years you and everyone else have ignored it because of her parents!"

"Jackie. Please!"

At that moment, in the middle of all the infighting Mr. Patterson has a flashback of Carlos on the morning of the Honor's Day program. He is reminded of him fumbling with his camera.

"What if she had to help?" Mr. Patterson interrupts. Everyone quiets down.

"Help, from who?" Diana asks.

"The morning of the honors' program, I happened to spot Carlos Jones messing around with a very expensive camera," he replies. "I didn't make much of it then."

"Who is he?" Diana asks.

"He is a menace who should be placed in resource," Mr. Patterson replies.

"Now, don't start that," Jackie interrupts. "I'm sick of every time a young black man has discipline issues, we are ready to place him in special needs or medicate him."

"He is a student at Riverside, and a pretty good athlete," Dr. Lanier responds. "You know. When I think about it, I did suspend him for leaving campus in Miss Banner's car. I remember he was pretty upset with me."

Everyone pauses to take it all in.

"So, what now?" Jackie asks.

"Now, I think I should pay Miss Banner a visit," Dr. Lanier replies. "Besides, I owe her a conversation. It was my idea to have her mentor Mrs. Meeks. It seems to me that I may have poured gasoline on the fire.

"Are you seriously going to visit her, now?" Jackie asks.

"Yes, Jackie. I'm very serious," he replies. "This can't simply wait to resolve itself."

"Well, I'm going with you," Mr. Patterson interrupts.

"No, please, let me handle it, James," Dr. Lanier replies.

"Oh, no. If it's true, then she owes us both an explanation."

"I can see you have your mind made up," Dr. Lanier says. "Fine. Then we should get going."

Everyone stands. Dr. Lanier walks over to Jackie and gives her a huge hug.

"Jackie, my oldest and dearest friend, thank you for watching my back."

"I've been watching it all these years; I can't stop now." she jokes.

"I'll get Caleb, Jackie," Diana says.

"You will do no such thing," Jackie replies. "You can get him tomorrow. Go home and work things out with Arthur."

Aunt Jackie ushers the three of them to the door.

＊＊＊＊

Dr. Lanier drives along, with Mr. Patterson in the passenger seat. Dr. Lanier dials a number using his cell phone only to get no answer. He looks over at Mr. Patterson who shrugs his shoulders.

"I will do a drive-by. Maybe she is in the shower," Dr. Lanier says.

Meanwhile, at Ruth's home, she and Carlos are cuddled on the couch watching television and smoking marijuana. Dr. Lanier pulls into Ruth's driveway. Drawn by curiosity at the bright headlights shining through her window, Ruth gets up to investigate. She peeps through the blinds.

"Shit!" she yells.

She begins fanning marijuana smoke.

"What's wrong!" Carlos shouts.

"It's Dr. Lanier!"

"What the hell is he doing here?" Carlos says.

"I don't know!" Ruth yells. "You got to hide!"

Carlos quickly grabs as many of his personal items as he can and then bolts for the back bedroom. Ruth frantically scans the room for more evidence. She grabs a can of air freshener from the bookshelf and begins spraying relentlessly. There is a knock at the door. She places the aerosol bottle on the shelf and pauses to gather herself.

"Just one second!" she yells out. She walks over and opens the door. "Dr. Lanier, Mr. Patterson, what are you two doing here?"

"Good evening, Miss Banner. I apologize for dropping by unannounced. I was wondering if I could have just a moment of your time?" Dr. Lanier asks.

"Well, Uh... I guess."

Inside the Bedroom, Carlos peeps through the bedroom door. He grimaces at the fact that Ruth allowed the men inside.

The men enter. They both squint and glance at one another as they are taken aback by the smell of what they believe to be a very poor attempt to mask marijuana smoke.

"Please, won't you both have a seat. Could I get you something?" a visibly nervous Ruth asks.

"I'll have a glass of water if you don't mind," Dr. Lanier says.

"Nothing for me," Mr. Patterson replies.

Ruth hurries off to the kitchen. Mr. Patterson notices an extra glass and a car magazine on the coffee table. He nudges Dr. Lanier's leg to make him aware.

"I didn't know you were into cars, Miss Banner," Dr. Lanier yells from the living room.

"Cars, sir?" She pauses. "Oh, yeah, I was thinking of getting a new car radio."

In the bedroom, Carlos hangs his head in disbelief that she would say that.

Ruth returns, and hands Dr. Lanier his glass, then takes a seat in her recliner.

"Thank you," Dr. Lanier says.

He makes room on the coffee table to place his glass. Inadvertently, he spots Carlos's state ring underneath one of the magazines.

"What's this?" he mumbles.

Ruth becomes paralyzed with fear, as Dr. Lanier slowly picks up the ring and begins reading the inscription. Mr. Patterson leans over, and they both read the inscription together. Both men simultaneously turn and stare at Ruth.

In the bedroom, Carlos looks down at his finger and realizes he is not wearing his ring.

"Oh shit!" he whispers.

Back in the living room, Ruth stutters. "I don't-

"Miss Banner, is Carlos here?" Dr. Lanier calmly interrupts.

Suddenly, Carlos appears behind Mr. Patterson, wielding a baseball bat.

"Carlos, don't!" Ruth shouts.

Before Mr. Patterson could react, Carlos strikes him in the head. He instantly falls to the floor. Carlos then targets Dr. Lanier. He takes aim and swings at his head, but Dr. Lanier raises his arms and partially blocks the blow. The tip of the bat slightly catches his forehead, and the force from the swing breaks his wrist.

Dr. Lanier is sprawled across the floor between the couch and coffee table. He slowly regains consciousness. His vision is blurred, but he can hear Ruth and Carlos's arguing. Careful not to alert the two of them, he reaches inside his pants pocket to retrieve his phone. He presses the call back button to dial the last incoming call from Jackie.

At Aunt Jackie's house, the phone rings.

"Hello."

She listens in horror at the chaotic chatter between Ruth and Carlos.

"What were you thinking Carlos!" Ruth yells.

"My father is going to kill me," he replies.

"Carlos! We have to get him to a doctor!"

"Son, listen to what she is telling you," a groggy Dr. Lanier interrupts from his position on the floor. "If Mr. Patterson dies, your father will be the least of your worries."

"Shut up! Everybody just shut up! Let me think," Carlos yells.

A horrified, Jackie immediately hangs up the phone and dials 911. She pauses. She realizes that she doesn't know where Ruth lives.

At Diana and Arthur's home, Diana and Miss Nelson are relaxing on the couple's couch, drinking wine. Both women are a little tipsy.

"Gay! I can't believe Jackie kept that kind of gossip from me," Miss Nelson shouts.

Diana laughs.

"Could you please stop reminding me?" Diana says as she takes a sip of wine.

Arthur enters the apartment. The women gather themselves.

"Hey," he humbly says.

Diana ignores him and rolls her eyes.

"Hello, Arthur," Miss Nelson replies.

Arthur takes a seat. For a second, everyone sits there in awkward silence.

"Well, I think I'll leave and let you two talk things over," Miss Nelson says.

She attempts to stand, gets dizzy, and falls back in a drunken slump onto the couch. She can't help but laugh at her own intoxicated condition.

"Oh no. You can't drive like this," Diana says. "You can sleep here tonight."

"She is right," Arthur responds.

"Huh, thank you," Diana snaps.

"I'm not staying here another second, if you two are just planning to ignore one another all night. Show him the pictures Miss Meeks," Miss Nelson admonishes.

"I've seen them already," Arthur replies.

Miss Nelson snatches the manila envelope from the coffee table and hands it to Arthur.

"You haven't seen these."

Arthur reluctantly opens the envelope and removes the photos. He is stunned by what he sees.

"What the hell is this?" he asks.

"That is one of many reasons why you should have known that I would never cheat on you," Diana interrupts. "I was supposed to meet Miss Banner at the restaurant, but he showed up before she arrived. I tried to explain before you stormed out."

He takes a long pause. He reflects and becomes embarrassed by his behavior.

"So, these two are gay?" Arthur asks.

"I know what you're thinking Arthur. It's always the pretty boys you don't expect," Miss Nelson replies.

Diana throws up her hands in frustration.

"Jesus Christ! Really? Is that the most important thing right now!"

Arthur, feeling remorseful tosses the photos across the table and reaches for her hand.

"Of course not, baby; I don't know what to say.

Diana's phone suddenly rings.

"Just save it." Diana reaches for the phone. "Hello. Jackie, slow down. I can't understand you."

Miss Nelson and Arthur look on with concern. Diana places her hand over the receiver. "Something has happened to Dr. Lanier," she explains.

"Miss Nelson is here with me. She knows the way. I'll call you with the address when we get there."

"We have to go!" Diana shouts.

"What's wrong, Diana!" Miss Nelson replies.

"I'll explain on the way."

They rush out of the door.

Outside Ruth's home, they sit in the car. Miss Nelson confirms the car parked in the driveway belongs to Dr. Lanier. Diana makes the call to Jackie.

"Jackie, the address is 3644 Cotton Wood. Call 911. We are going in," she says. They all exit the vehicle and hurry across the street.

Seconds later, Miss Nelson knocks at Ruth's door. Anxious seconds go by. Slowly, the door opens. With the chain latched, Ruth peeps through the crack. Inside, Carlos stands behind the door wielding the bat. Dr. Lanier is on the floor fully conscious, but in severe pain. A critically injured Mr. Patterson is stretched out on the floor nearby.

"Ruth, let us inside. Miss Nelson demands. "Where is Dr. Lanier?"

A relieved Dr. Lanier hears her voice and screams out, "Help!"

Arthur jumps into action. He shoves Diana and Miss Nelson aside. He then braces and rams his shoulder into the center of the door. Ruth quickly moves aside for fear of being hit by the force of the door. The chain snaps. Ruth screams. Arthur forces his way inside past her. Suddenly, with his bat raised, Carlos attempts to strike Arthur from behind.

"Arthur watch out!" Diana shouts.

Arthur turns, just in time, and stops the attack. He and Carlos violently struggle as he attempts to remove the bat from his Carlos's grip. Miss Nelson and Diana hurry to the aid of Dr. Lanier and Mr. Patterson. Arthur finally overwhelms Carlos and takes possession of the bat. He gives Carlos a few vicious blows to the face; breaking his will to fight any longer.

"I'm just a kid!" Carlos shouts.

"Baby, that's enough!" Diana yells.

Miss Nelson frantically attempts to stop the blood pouring from Mr. Patterson's head. Diana assists Dr. Lanier from the floor. She helps lift him onto the couch.

"Get me more towels," Miss Nelson yells to Diana.

Diana sprints out of the room. Ruth slumps down in her chair and cups her head inside the palm of her hands. Arthur stands guard with the bat over a defeated Carlos.

Diana returns with the towels. She hands them to Miss Nelson.

"He needs a doctor now," Miss Nelson shouts.

"Help should be here soon," Diana replies.

Extremely upset, Diana steps back to gather her emotions. She inadvertently steps on Carlos's open gym bag lying in the corner. She turns to investigate. Noticing the camera and a manila envelope, Diana stoops down and removes the items. She immediately turns to Ruth.

"Jackie was right. It was you," she says.

In a fit of paranoia, Ruth leaps to her feet and launches at Diana. She snatches the folder from her hand.

"Give me that!" she screams.

Her aggression causes the photos to fall to the floor, revealing incriminating evidence which include among photos of Dr. Lanier and Mr., Patterson, pictures of Miss Nelson and Coach Curry having sex in the library. Everyone is stunned. Ruth quickly turns to Miss Nelson.

"Those were for Coach Bea and not you. I didn't know what his plans were. I just needed extra assurance that he wouldn't apply for the job" she explains.

"Well, you certainly had all the bases covered Ruth," a stunned Miss Nelson replies. She shakes her head.

"None of this would have happened if was not for you!" Ruth yells at Diana. She then turns to Dr. Lanier. "The only reason you brought her here is because she is black."

"Excuse me!" Diana interrupts. "I was recruited because I earned the right to be here!"

"Ladies, please stop! Dr. Lanier interrupts. "No, Dr. Lanier! She needs to hear this. You see, Miss Banner, some of us had to work hard to get the things we want out of life. I didn't have Daddy's trust fund or Mama's connections."

"How dare you! You don't know a damn thing about me!" Ruth screams. "I love that school, and those kids more than you ever could. I deserve to be principal!"

Diana turns her attention to Carlos who is still sprawled on the floor and being guarded by Arthur.

"If this is your idea of loving the kids, then maybe you're right Miss Banner. You deserve the job a lot more than me. You've proven you're certainly willing do a hell of a lot more for it."

"That's enough!" Dr. Lanier shouts. He turns to Ruth. "Miss Banner, are these photos the only ones left? Answer me, dammit!"

"Yes!"

Just then, police sirens can be heard in the near distance. Seconds later, blue lights reflect through the window.

"Mrs. Meeks, please pack everything inside that bag and take it with you," Dr. Lanier orders.

"What!" she shouts.

"Just do it!"

Diana shakes her head in disgust, but she reluctantly complies with his request.

"Nothing about the photos leaves this room," he says. "Riverside does not need a scandal on top of everything else. Does everyone understand?"

Everyone is stunned by the Dr. Lanier's candor, but they all comply.

Police and paramedics enter the home. The officers gently place Ruth in handcuffs, and aggressively remove Carlos from the floor and place him in handcuffs. The paramedics quickly attend to Mr. Patterson as Ruth and Carlos are escorted out.

A few weeks later, in the lobby of Riverside, a large picture of Mr. Patterson hangs on the wall. A message underneath reads, "Get well soon, we miss you."

Inside her office, Diana sits at her desk, reading her emails.

"Can I come in?" a male voice interrupted.

She raises her head and pushes her glasses up on her face to get a clearer look. She gives a tentative smile that builds over the surprise of seeing Dr. Lanier standing there.

"Hey you!" she shouts. "Of course, you can come in."

Dr. Lanier smiles and enters the office. She stands and walks over to him to give him a hug. She is keenly aware of his injured head and bandaged wrist. She gingerly embraces him. Dr. Lanier takes a seat in-front of the desk. Diana returns to her chair.

"So, is everyone treating you ok?" He asks.

"Everyone has been wonderful," she replies.

"Good, I'm happy to hear it."

The two of them sit in awkward silence for a second. The recent drama still fresh in their minds causes extreme discomfort and they don't really know where to start the conversation.

"So how —"

---How are... I'm sorry, you go ahead," Diana says.

"I was going to ask about Arthur and Caleb?" Dr. Lanier says.

"Caleb is great. Arthur and I are getting better. We are in counseling," she replies. "I've decided, or should I say, we've decided that he should start his own computer repair business."

"Really? That's great!"

"Well, financially it's been a challenge, but Aunt Jackie has been a God-send. She and Caleb are inseparable, and she refuses to take a dime for watching him. Can you believe that?" she asks.

"No kidding?" he replies. "Good old Jackie, she is something."

They endure another long awkward pause. Diana puts on a pasted smile, and Dr. Lanier clears his throat.

"You know, Mrs. Meeks, I really wish this whole thing didn't go down the way it did," Dr. Lanier humbly says.

"Let me be clear Dr. Lanier. I don't blame you for what happened," she replies.

"Well, I thank you for saying that." He chuckles. "I would not have blamed you and Arthur if you all had packed up your things and high-tailed it back to Dallas."

Diana nervously laughs.

"I can't say that the thought never entered my mind. So, how have you been?" she asks.

"Retirement is good," he replies. "Putting the pieces of my life back together at my age is another story."

"I can't imagine. I heard Mr. Patterson has really made a strong recovery," Diana says.

"Yes, thank God. He is doing quite well. It's hard to believe with the injuries he suffered. God is good."

"Amen," she replies.

"Mrs. Meeks, I'm just going to come right out and say it. I know that you didn't agree with the way in which I handled the situation that night," Dr. Lanier says.

"Listen, you did what you believed was right," she replies. "At first, yes. I had a hard time with it." She reaches for his hand. "It was a tough decision, but I respect it. God knows I would not have wanted to be in your shoes."

He surrenders his hand to her.

"Thank you," he says. "I sure hit the lottery when I found you. You're going to make a fine administrator." He releases her hand and stands. "Well, I know you have work to do, and I don't want to take up too much of your time. "If you need anything, please don't hesitate to give me a call."

"Thank you. I will."

Dr. Lanier turns to exit. He stops and takes one last view of his old office. Diana leans back in her chair. She cups her elbow and taps her lip with her index finger.

"Dr. Lanier, I don't know why I care, but what the heck. " she says.

"Yes; what is it? "he replies.

"Just out of curiosity, what became of those two?" she asks.

He hesitates for a second.

"Well, I spoke with Carlos's father not too long ago, and he seems to be very pleased with his son's progress. It appears confinement has given him time to reflect on his mistakes. The young man could have a bright future after all."

"Good for him. Is there any news on Miss Banner? Has she resurfaced?" Diana asks.

"You know. I'm not sure. But if there is one thing I do know, with her mother around, she is almost guaranteed to land on her feet," he replies.

Across town, at Shady Oaks Charter School, Ruth is being escorted by a very enthusiastic Principal Tillman. His obvious attraction to her is overwhelming. He can't help but walk closely beside her. Sensing his violation of her space, Ruth attempts to create distance by constantly shifting her stance. Not to encourage him, she avoids eye contact.

"You're going to love it here at Shady Oaks, Miss Banner. I was very excited when Mother told me you were interested in the position," he says.

"Is that so?" she replies while giving him a forced smile.

Ruth's attention is diverted by the well-behaved students dressed in uniform as they pass class.

"Is everything alright?" Principal Tillman asks.

"Oh, yes sir. I am very excited. Thank you for the opportunity," she embellishes.

Principal Tillman places his hand on her shoulder and ushers her to a nearby set of double doors.

"If you come this way Miss Banner, I want to show you our state-of-the-art gymnasium."

Just before entering the corridor that leads to the gymnasium, an African American male student approaches the two of them from behind.

"Good morning Principal Tillman," the young man says.

Slightly startled, he turns around.

"Good morning Tyrique!" Principal Tillman replies. He taps Ruth on her shoulder. "Miss Banner, I would like you to meet Tyrique Cooper. He is one of our brightest students."

Ruth turns and, in an instant, becomes awestruck by the handsome young man.

"Please to meet you Miss Banner," Tyrique says. He extends his hand.

"The pleasure is all mine Tyrique," she replies.

Ruth quickly grabs a hold and cradles his hand. She stares intimately into his eyes. Awkward seconds pass with Ruth completely distracted by Tyrique's presence. The inappropriate behavior causes Tyrique slight discomfort. It forces Principal Tillman to intervene. He clears his throat.

"Well, I think we should finish the tour. Hurry to class, Tyrique," he admonishes.

Ruth reluctantly releases Tyrique's hand, and he the young man quickly dismisses himself. Principal Tillman grabs her arm and again attempts to usher her toward the gymnasium. As the two of them proceed down the corridor A deep male voice suddenly stops them.

"Excuse me, Principal Tillman," the man says.

"Yes," Principal Tillman replies.

He turns. Standing there alongside a uniformed police officer, are Carlos's parents.

"My name is Edward Jones, and this is my wife Frances. We would like to have a word with you," Edward says.

Ruth slowly turns; her eyes widen, and she gasps, while trying desperately to hold back her scream.

The End